Light in the Evening Time

LaJoyce Martin

Light in the Evening Time

by LaJoyce Martin

©1995, Word Aflame Press
Hazelwood, MO 63042-2299
Printing History: 1996

Cover design by Paul Povolni
Cover Art by Bill Myers

All Scripture quotations in this book are from the King James Version of the Bible unless otherwise identified.

Printed in United States of America

Printed by

Library of Congress Cataloging-in-Publication Data

Martin, LaJoyce, 1937–
    Light in the evening time / by LaJoyce Martin.
        p.   cm.
    ISBN 1-56722-132-7
    I. Title.
PS3563.A72486L53   1995
813'.54dc20   95-19684
                                                                    CIP

Light in the Evening Time

To

My Future Son-in-Law.

Whoever and wherever you are,

Would you please call my daughter?

Contents

CHAPTER ONE

The Revelation

"**D**on't leave me, Ma! I'll have nowhere to go!"

Even as her desperation forged the words, Cathy realized their uselessness. The only link with her past was descending the steps to a beckoning grave.

"Go . . . to . . . your . . . father . . ." The syllables staggered out through thin, blue lips. It was Cathy's first sight of the skeleton Catherine Willis had hidden in the closet more than fourteen years earlier.

"I have a *father?*"

"Yes."

Some secret, dark and off limits to questioning, had kept the girl from any knowledge of the circumstances that surrounded her birth. She didn't even know her father's name.

"But, Ma, you never told me—"

"Your . . . mother died. I'm your . . . grandmother."

Catherine's breathing slowed, and her eyes slid shut. Cathy thought she was gone. With no further information, how would she ever know who she was? And how should she find a man she had just learned existed?

Catherine Willis was a fighter. She had fought against

everything all her life: the loss of both parents, a young and fleeting marriage, a disease that left her scarred, and poverty. Added to this was her only daughter's determination to wed Ed Dillingham, a penniless woodcutter. She fought the union blindly and without rules—and succeeded only in alienating her son-in-law from herself.

It wasn't fair that her own beautiful Lia, for whom she held such high hopes as an artist, should be saddled with an insensitive lout of a husband. Catherine said so, and Ed Dillingham invited her out of their lives. That's why she wasn't there when her granddaughter was born.

Now, as Catherine lay dying, her past came into crisp focus in one brief flashback. Five years of silent stubbornness had kept a gaping chasm between her and her disfavored son-in-law. Neither was willing to go around it by the path of forgiveness. When it came to the showdown, Lia's full allegiance went to Ed, a factor that Catherine should have anticipated but didn't. The letters that Catherine wrote to her daughter were all returned unopened.

When Lia lay in a coma, though, Ed had softened and sent word for Catherine to come. When she arrived at Cranfills Gap, he was hardly civil to her, giving her no details of Lia's misfortune. These she learned from a neighbor who introduced herself as Mabel, an over-dressed woman with two fussy children clinging to her skirts.

"I've been most anxious for you to get here," the impatient lady said, warning the oldest child, a boy, to "sit down and clam up." "I'm afraid we're in for a long spell."

"What happened to Lia?" demanded Catherine.

"Ed and I figure that she tried to get up to fix the baby some onion tea and fainted. She hit her head on the iron stove and has not awakened since. Some rally and some don't, the doctor said."

Fearing that the noisy children would bother Lia and her newborn, Catherine insisted that Mabel take her children home at once and not return unless she could come alone and quietly.

The woman started to say more, but Catherine put her finger to her lips and ushered her to the door.

Catherine tried to hold Lia's soul in the land of the living, but all her efforts were futile. When Lia died, Catherine folded her daughter's arms across her chest, put a penny on each of her eyelids, and fled in the night with her tiny granddaughter. She resolved to fight every agency, law—or the devil himself—to keep the baby. The child was all she had left of Lia . . . of *anything*.

If her conscience pricked her over kidnapping the child, no one knew it. She convinced herself that, left with Ed Dillingham, the child would not have survived anyhow.

Catherine moved to a remote area and made no further contact with Ed. She changed the baby's name from Edna to Cathy, gave the baby her own maiden name, and closed the door on the past.

"*Where?* Where is my father, and how shall I find him?" Cathy's beseeching words braided together fear, helplessness, and a plea. She had a father somewhere, and the thought so stretched her mind that it could not return to its original proportions. "Oh, Ma! Ma!" Panic tore at her throat. "Please talk to me!"

Catherine's eyelids fluttered. "Ed . . . Dillingham. Ticket . . . purse." The words were barely audible. Then with one long, shuddering breath, she was gone, taking the fourteen years of silence with her.

Ed Dillingham. Cathy repeated the strange-sounding name over and over for fear it would slip away. What would her father look like? Would he have large, chunky hands like the man at the general store? A brownish red beard? Would he have brown eyes like her own? Could a daughter bear the favor of a father, or was that right exclusive to male children? Did girls resemble their mothers only? Cathy's brows knit in study. The more she deliberated, the more confused she became. *Cathy Dillingham.* She said the name aloud and liked the way it rolled around on her tongue.

Her "ma" was dead, and grief was on its way. Cathy sensed its approach, but she set up a roadblock against it long enough to search through her grandmother's purse for an answer. She couldn't cut one lifeline without having another to grasp. If she did, she would surely sink. An hour ago, she was Cathy Willis. Now she was Cathy Dillingham. She felt dangled somewhere between the two.

She found the ticket, but it gave her no insight as to her destination. She couldn't read the codes. She didn't know what "Crfl/Gp" or "Tx" meant. She must trust a deceased woman and an unknown coach driver to get her to . . . wherever.

In the bottom of the purse was a scrap of paper that said: *Don, I have forgiven you.* She was sure that her grandmother had said *Ed.* It was all too complex to unravel, requiring a tariff that her mind couldn't pay.

Cathy's young body, deprived too long of rest and goaded beyond its strength, begged for respite. She dropped beside the bed on which the corpse lay and fell into a deep sleep. Cold crept into the room and into Catherine Willis's lifeless form as the sun lowered itself in the west.

A bold knock at the door brought the girl to her senses. It took a minute for her to remember why she was kneeling beside the bed and to contemplate her present distress. Ma was dead and must be buried! The fire had gone out in the wood stove; Cathy shivered with a chill that went past her skin and reached her spirit.

Unbarring the door, she peered into the face of the landowner's wife. Ruth Gomer was a dour woman whose milk of human kindness had clabbered. Catherine once said she had "a nose for everybody's business and a tongue long enough to stir trouble like a churn dasher." Cathy, as a child, was terrified of Mrs. Gomer's evil temperament. She wondered how one so devoid of spiritual fruit merited a Bible name.

Mr. Gomer's name was Percival, and Catherine's favorite quotation was "May God have mercy on Percy." He was a good man but rather dense, oblivious to his wife's duplicity. He believed anything Ruth said without unwrapping it to see what was on the inside. She handled all the financial affairs to her own advantage.

The stucco hut that Cathy's grandmother rented from the Gomers could hardly be called a house. The one oblong room that answered the treble purpose of kitchen, parlor, and bedroom worked vainly to keep the elements at bay. As the structure deteriorated, Ruth Gomer refused to finance the repairs—or to lower the rent. She knew that Catherine Willis had nowhere else to go and no money to get her there.

Ruth huffed into the room, pushing Cathy aside. She stopped short at the sight of the still remains on the bed. "She's—she's *dead?*"

"Yes'm."

"I can't believe that Catherine up and died without finishing my antimacassars," she sputtered. "That was part of the rent agreement, that she'd do my needlework."

Cathy said nothing.

"When did she expire?"

"Just . . . a little while ago."

"We'll have to call the mortician to come and lay her out."

"Yes'm."

"You'll have to stay here with her until the burial."

"Yes'm."

"Can't you say anything but yes'm?"

"I'm sorry—" Cathy lowered her eyes in shame at the rebuke.

"Then when we get her in the ground," continued Ruth, "I'll clean out the cabin and—" She started to say more but clamped her teeth together. "Well, first things first."

CHAPTER TWO

Lost Ticket

The undertaker came directly. He asked if there were any relatives to be contacted, and Cathy said no. To mention that there was an Ed Dillingham whose whereabouts were unknown would only complicate matters.

"I'm glad to find the room so cool," said the mortician. "That way the body will be less likely to bloat. I'll be back in the morning with the burial box." He turned to go. "And where will you go after the funeral?"

"My grandmother arranged for my care before she died."

"I'm gladsome," he said. "The poor farm is no place for a young lady like you."

The poor farm? Cathy's cheeks turned crimson at the implied atrocity. She had heard horrifying stories about the place. Had her grandmother died before imparting the precious information about her father, would she have gone to the *poor farm?* The prospect was too terrible to consider.

Rationality was shrouded with a foggy vapor. Memories of yesterday amalgamated with uncertainties of tomorrow, and nothing was clear. Cathy's body moved machine like without the participation of her mind.

She had much to do. What little her grandmother possessed must be packed for the journey or sold. She would take only the more valuable things along with her: her grandmother's emerald brooch, the handmade quilts, and the paintings. The bed, table, and chairs she would sell; they wouldn't bring much, but it would give her a small sum for food until she reached her father's house.

However, as Cathy turned to leave the grave the next day, Mrs. Gomer stepped in front of her, blocking her way. "Your ma was behind on the rent," she said.

"I remember . . . that she paid it."

"But she did not finish the sewing, and the sewing was part of the rent. Therefore, whatever she had when she passed away now belongs to me."

"The quilts—"

"You may have *one* quilt to take with you to the poor farm. Everything else will go to cover the unpaid rent."

"The *poor farm?*"

"Where else do you think you would go, Cathy? *I* certainly don't intend to adopt you. You're neither old enough nor strong enough to earn your keep."

"I'm going to my father."

"To your father?"

"Yes'm. Ed Dillingham." Cathy squared her skimpy shoulders. Childhood had taken wings; she was now a young woman. "I'm not really Cathy *Willis* at all. I'm Cathy *Dillingham.* Catherine was my *grandmother.*"

"Now that's a likely story! And where does your father live?"

"I . . . I don't know—yet."

Ruth Gomer stabbed at Cathy with her sharp eyes. "Then how, pray tell, shall you go to your father if you don't even know where he is?"

"Ma—that is, Catherine—took care of that before she passed on. She purchased a stagecoach ticket for me that will take me directly to my father. I have it in the purse here."

Ruth's eyes took on an avaricious and calculating fire. "She did, eh?"

Cathy didn't flinch. "Yes'm."

"In that case, you will give me the ticket, and I shall get a refund. That will help cover the funeral expenses. Morticians don't work for free, nor do I provide lodging for free." She held out her hand for the purse.

When Cathy refused to relinquish the handbag, Mrs. Gomer snatched it from her, almost knocking Cathy off her feet. The girl's world reeled.

The mortician had been watching. "What is going on here?" he asked, his attention traveling from Ruth to Cathy and back again.

"The little villain took my purse!" lied Mrs. Gomer.

"I—I—"

"Please make allowances for her recent distress, madam," the undertaker urged. "She is scarce more than a child." He looked at Cathy. "And a very frightened one at that." He hurried on before Cathy could defend herself against Mrs. Gomer's falsehood.

"Go to the cabin and get your quilt, and I will be there in an hour to take you to the poorhouse," ordered Mrs. Gomer, her voice as hard as tempered steel.

It was too much. Cathy felt she would rather crawl into the grave with her grandmother than go to the

17

poorhouse where people were starved and demoralized. Catherine had pinched pennies to buy a ticket so that her granddaughter would have a place to go. Now, the worst had happened. . . .

Cathy couldn't stop the tears that threatened to drown even her heart. Her mind rebelled against parting with the scant comforts she had known. Every cracked teacup and ironstone bowl seemed precious. Why must Ruth Gomer demand *everything* for the sake of a few pennies of unpaid rent?

An hour! One short hour! Ruth Gomer would be coming to claim anything that Cathy didn't wear on her body. A sense of self-preservation took over, and Cathy donned all three of her dresses, two petticoats, and a sweater before overlaying the lot with her winter coat. She chose the warmest and prettiest quilt to take with her. Upon whatever shore of life she found herself cast, the quilt would be a thing of sentiment. Oh, and she'd want the special spoon for a keepsake—the one monogrammed with an "E." She ripped a small hole in the lining of her coat and hid it there. Lastly, she stuffed three linen handkerchief's bordered with Catherine's handmade hairpin lace into her pocket.

Mrs. Gomer came promptly on time. She didn't seem to notice Cathy's extra layers of clothing, but she seized the quilt from the girl's arms. "Not *that* quilt! It will bring a fair sum on the market. Take an older one. Here." She pulled a ragged quilt from the quilt box and shoved it toward Cathy. "You should be grateful for this. It is only because of my generosity that you're not going away empty-handed." Her eyes halted at the pin on Cathy's coat. "And what is that?"

Cathy realized too late that she had forgotten to put the brooch out of sight. "Ma's emerald brooch."

"I'll have that, too."

When they arrived at the poor farm, Mrs. Gomer waved—or signaled—to someone in the upper story window. She gave Cathy a condescending smile. "I hope that you will always remember Ruth Gomer as the charitable soul who provided a roof over your head and went the extra mile to see that you were properly placed in a care facility when you had nowhere else to go." Her smile took on the essence of a sneer. "It was noble of your grandmother to invent her grand fiction, but, of course, you must know that you have no father at all. If you did, he would have showed up long before now. I expect that the coach ticket is a part of the fabrication, too—and that it will prove quite worthless to me."

Cathy stumbled from the wagon clutching her tattered coverlet. She said nothing and dared not look back. Ruth Gomer would not have the satisfaction of seeing her tears.

CHAPTER THREE

The Poor Farm

Miss Weems, matron of the women at the farm, poked at Cathy's ribs. "Your arms and legs are skinny, but your middle is fat. We'll give you enough work to remove some of that excess blubber."

"I have on three dresses," Cathy said, innocently enough.

"Three dresses!"

"All of my clothes are on my back. I brought no grip-sack."

"Young lady, *nobody* has three dresses here. It isn't permitted. You will come down from your high horse and live like the rest of us. You will be allowed to keep one dress and donate the others to the institution for those less fortunate than yourself."

What more could be stripped from her Cathy did not know. She hoped that her grandmother, floating somewhere in eternity, could not divine her deplorable end. As for her father—if indeed he did exist—she had given up hope of ever seeing him.

Could Ruth Gomer be right? Was her grandmother incoherent when she mentioned Ed Dillingham? A father would surely make an effort to contact his own child in the space of fourteen years.

Conditions at the poorhouse were worse than Cathy could have imagined, worse than the stories she'd heard at school. The food did little to dissipate hunger. Servings of watery broth lacked proper nourishment, and dysentery was rampant among the residents.

The homeless, poor, sick, and insane huddled together in frightened clusters waiting for some immortal deliverance, though most realized that any illusion of rescue was but a pipe dream.

Pallets lined the floor end to end for sleeping. The men's dormitory was separated from the women's by a thin wall, but there was no age distinction in either room. All their eyes looked so old that it was impossible to determine any adult's age.

One morning as Cathy said her prayers, a wizened woman elbowed her. "Think God's a-hearin', eh? Lemme tell ye, kid, when you've been here as long as me, ye learn nobody listens or cares. God's done fergot this heap of blighted humanity." She lowered her voice and looked about cautiously. "That's why old man Jerden killed hisself yestiday."

"Ma'am, it isn't God's fault that we are here," Cathy said, striving to stave off the bitterness that clawed at her soul. "Circumstances of life put us in this miserable place. Even Jesus had no place to lay His head. This might be our chance to share in the fellowship of His suffering. Ma said that if we suffer with Him, we'll also be with Him in a glorious resurrection.

"Ma—she was really my grandmother—died, and I was cheated out of my rights. But if I never leave here, there's another world afterwards. And, oh, won't it look grand after spending a lifetime in want of a home?"

"Once I believed like you. But now I'm drained of ever' shred of my believin'. This dump has a way of scrapin' your spirit bone-bare."

"I'll be glad to say a prayer for you."

"Spare your breath, kid. I'm too brittle to care any more."

Cathy prayed again that night; praying helped her keep her sanity. As she drifted off to a restless sleep, she heard the whimper of a child. "Please, Mary, I'm cold . . ."

"Get away, you brat! Don't you put your cold feet on me!" a voice hissed.

The child moved from one bedroll to another. "No, Bonny, you can't sleep with me, either," another voice rasped. "I've told you before."

When she came to Cathy's pallet, Cathy pulled the shivering child under her ragged quilt. Thereafter, the frail orphan shared Cathy's cover while Cathy whispered Bible stories to her until she fell asleep, diverting her mind from the racking coughs and weary groans about them.

Cathy's first job was digging grubs for fish bait with the other younger residents. She loathed the work! The worms were cold and slimy and slipped away from her more often than not. The shaggy-haired boy who toiled beside her insisted on offering suggestions.

"Chief Bates says we're to put a hundred worms in a jar, but don't do it. Seventy or eighty will be plenty. He'll never count them. He wouldn't dirty his hands to touch a worm! If you put less in each jar, you can turn in more jars and you'll get a better rating."

"That would be dishonest," Cathy replied.

The boy hooted. *"Dishonest?* Who cares? Honesty will get you nowhere here."

"But I have to be true to myself. To my conscience. To God."

"I can tell that *you're* a greenhorn here."

"I'd rather die than lie."

He shrugged. "As you will. I'll choose to turn in more jars. Everybody does. The bait shop pays by the jar. A penny each."

"To *us*?"

"Are you kidding? If you stay here a hundred years, you'll never see a copper. Everything goes in Chief Bates's pocket. At least you're old enough to remember what a coin looks like."

"Does anyone get out of here for any reason?"

"Not females."

"Couldn't someone adopt the little ones like Bonny?"

"If they knew about her, maybe. The government pays per person, and Chief doesn't want to lose any of his revenue. Therefore, he doesn't advertise that there are children here—and discourages anyone who would come looking. That would be money out of his pocket!"

"Why couldn't a woman leave when she's grown up?"

"She'd have no money or no home. If she had home and money, she wouldn't be here in the first place. Oh, I guess she could get married, but who would come to a poorhouse looking for a *wife*?"

"If I knew where my father was, I would send word to him and he'd come for me." It might be wishful thinking, but saying it made Cathy feel better.

24

"Even if you knew his address, you couldn't get word to him."

"Why not? This isn't a prison, is it?"

"Where would you get paper or a stamp? Chief wouldn't give it to you because he wants you here as his merchandise. You're making him money."

Hopelessness bit deep. To think that she might still be here when she was old and bent sent a sickness surging through Cathy's stomach. She staunched a gag.

"And if you don't start stuffing grubs in that jar, you'll end up working in the scullery, which is worse than a dungeon. This is the easy job."

True to the boy's prediction, Cathy didn't meet her quota of worms and was relegated to the kitchen. It reeked with filth and the smell of greasy cabbage; rodents crawled in and around everything. Nothing was wasted, regardless of its weevil content. Hours that started before daybreak and stretched until after dark imparted such pain in Cathy's legs that they cramped unmercifully. What little appetite she had took a plunge.

Days of sunlight and shadow passed with monotonous sameness. Faces blurred and swam in her ocean of despair. Cathy gave little attention to those around her, but one young man watched her with such hungry eyes that she felt uneasy. She had never seen him work and wondered that he got by with idleness.

"How old are you?" he demanded one day, following her into the kitchen.

"Scaring fifteen." Cathy turned back to the big, black stove.

"Talk to me!" he barked.

"I'm busy."

"That doesn't matter. What is your name?"

"Cathy Willis. I mean Cathy Dillingham."

"You're married?"

"No."

"Then why did you change your name?"

"It's none of your business."

Miss Weems passed the door, and Cathy whirled back to the pot she was attending, sure that she would be disciplined for talking. Her mouth went dry, her knees weak.

"Ha! Are you scared of old hawkeye?" The boy gave a foul laugh. "As long as *I'm* here, she won't bother you. She wouldn't dare." His base eyes grew brighter. "By the way, my name is Keeper."

"A stupid name."

He roared with laughter, causing his stomach to shake. "You said it, dolly! It is most stupid! There's a story behind my name that is just as dumb as the name itself. Pa used to fish. When he'd catch a scrawny fish, he'd throw it back. But when he would catch a fine one, he'd keep it. When I was born, he said I was a 'keeper.' The name stuck." He snatched a biscuit from the bread pan and began to munch on it.

"You mustn't steal bread," Cathy scolded. "There's none to spare. Little Bonny cries for more every night."

"Who is *little* Bonny?"

"A child in my quarters."

"Then take her some bread."

"That wouldn't be honest."

"Honest? If *I* say you can have extra bread, then you can. There's nothing dishonest about it."

"You don't run this place."

26

"My pa does. He makes big bucks. Have you ever heard of the poor law?"

Cathy shook her head.

"It's been here since the Pilgrims, but in 1834 it was placed under the national government. Pa gets a fat check from them every month. Four dollars a head."

"I'm not interested in history *or* in your father's wealth." Caught in a cyclone of dismay and loathing, Cathy spat the words. "I think it is a *crime* to use human beings for gain!"

"But I am interested in *you*, Dolly. Remember, my name is Keeper, and when I find a gal I like, I keep 'er!" He guffawed.

"Go away!"

"If you'll cooperate with me, you can have anything you want."

"Cooperate?"

His unquenchable lust leaped to life. "You're not *that* innocent. You know what I mean."

"I'd rather starve than be a . . . . a . . ."

"Oh, don't say a bad word, Miss Lily White. It might soil your holy mouth." He reached out and pinched her cheek.

Disregarding his advantage of five years and a hundred pounds over her, Cathy gave him a hostile shove, catching him off guard. He sprawled across the floor, overturning a cask of pickling brine that splattered in his eyes and covered his face.

The physical challenge incited his evil nature. "Wow! I like your spunk! And you'll get your come uppance."

"Come back and I'll give you more of the same."

"Dip out some of that soup before the water goes in

27

and fatten yourself up, kitten. Those muscles will be stronger. And I'll be back for more." He wiped the salty liquid from his face and left chuckling.

Dear God, Cathy flung the silent prayer toward heaven, *please get me out of here before I lose my mind and my honor. . . .*

CHAPTER FOUR

No Refund

A deafening crack, like the shot of a cannon, sent Ruth Gomer flying to the window in alarm. "What was that awful noise, Percy?"

"Lightning struck close by."

He joined her, pointing toward the eastern horizon. "Look! It's the rent house that was hit!" Fingers of fire leaped toward the sky. "The roof is burning like dry cedar!" He grabbed for his boots; his face twisted in panic. "The girl—!"

"Cathy isn't there."

"You are sure, Ruth?"

"Yes. I took her in the wagon to—"

"Oh, thank God!" He slumped into a chair. "She is safe."

"But the furnishings—the quilts—Catherine's paintings—!"

Percival Gomer shook his head. "I'm afraid nothing can be saved, Ruth. There will be nothing left for the girl but ashes."

"The contents of the house didn't belong to Cathy anyhow."

"What do you mean?"

"Catherine Willis gave me all that was left behind to clear up the rent."

"The rent?"

"Yes, Percival." Her child-placating tone suggested he was a small boy to whom trifles must be explained. "Besides the money Catherine paid monthly, she sewed for me in exchange for her lodging. She hadn't been able to sew for some weeks."

"As dilapidated as the old place was, you should have let her stay without charge, Ruth."

"No, Percy, that would have made her an object of charity and taken away her human dignity. No woman likes that. You don't understand *women*. The more you charge them for an item—be it apparel or be it a fee—the more *self-worth* they feel."

"That doesn't make sense. The widow was barely scrimping along with her little daughter—"

Another clap of thunder jolted the earth. "Percival, this is unusual weather for this time of year, isn't it? Thunder and lightning and storms?"

"Yes, Ruth, it is. But we're living in the last and evil days, and the Good Book speaks of the elements raging. It didn't specify that the winter would be exempt from that raging, either. It's just another sign of the end of time. Ruth, are you ready for the world to melt with fervent heat?"

A visible tremor passed through Ruth's stout frame. "I—I don't know. I've been extraordinarily good, Percy— and generous to a fault. I gave that orphan granddaughter of Catherine's a nice quilt, and I offered her transportation to the poor farm *in our own wagon!*"

"To the poor farm? You took that little girl to *the poor farm?*"

"Why, yes, Percy. I expect that's where Catherine would have wanted her to go. Where else would she live? And she's not *little*. She's on the brink of womanhood, and we certainly couldn't keep her here on *our* pitiful income. Besides, no house is large enough for two women. Shakespeare, the wisest man on earth, said that himself."

"Solomon was the wisest man who ever lived," corrected Mr. Gomer.

"Can't you do anything but argue, Percival? What does it matter who said it? It's true."

"Surely there could have been *some* other place for the girl."

"There you go arguing again! There wasn't." She cast a nervous glance at the window, bracing for another clap of thunder. "Oh, Catherine tried to keep Cathy from *knowing* her destination, to be sure. She even invented a preposterous story about the girl having a father alive somewhere. Wasn't that clever?"

"Catherine's husband?"

"Catherine wasn't Cathy's mother, Percy. She was her grandmother. I had already decided that and a passel of other things, too. When Catherine first came, I said to myself, says I, 'That woman is too old to have a small baby.' But not to be judgmental or nosy, I kept quiet about it even though I smelled a rat as big as the barn it lived in!"

"And you're saying that she has a *father?*"

"*I'm* saying no such. For whatever reason, Catherine led the girl to believe that she had a nice place to go after

Catherine passed herself on to the beyond. She took the tale so far as to provide a fake coach ticket for Cathy's trip!"

"If Mrs. Willis couldn't even pay the nominal rent you charged her, she certainly couldn't have bought a coach fare."

"That's my point exactly. And so I did something very noble to spare Cathy a bitter disappointment. I asked for the ticket to help defray the funeral expenses. I told Cathy that I would get a refund on the fare and apply that to the cost of the wooden box. That way, she could feel that she shared in the proper laying away of her grandmother—and she will never have to know that the ticket is a worthless piece of paper. Her memory of her beloved grandmother will be untarnished by Catherine's innocent fabrication."

"You are indeed a unique woman, Ruth. You think of everything."

"Thank you, dear Percy. A wife likes to hear words of praise now and then." She sighed deeply. "But now the rent house and everything in it is lost, taking that income away."

"I'm glad the shack is gone. It wasn't fit for human habitation."

"I do have Catherine's emerald brooch, though. It is quite valuable."

"Why should you have her brooch, Ruth?"

"She gave it to me as a token of friendship. I *did* try to befriend her, and she appreciated my kindness. Do you remember the time I took her that sorghum, Percy?"

"The syrup that was so badly burned I couldn't eat it?"

"Catherine especially liked overcooked sorghum. And

as I was saying, Catherine knew there'd be funeral expenses and—"

"I thought the *county* buried Mrs. Willis."

Ruth detoured his remark. "The emerald is quite an expensive piece. I should like to know where she got it."

"It seems to me that the girl should have the brooch, Ruth. If it is so costly, she could have sold it and stayed out of the poorhouse for a few days. Surely she could have found a job as a governess or a maid."

Ruth squirmed; Percival was getting close to her villainy. "You don't think the world will end today, do you, Percy?"

"I wouldn't be a bit surprised, Ruth."

However, when the storm abated, so did Ruth Gomer's sense of conviction. She assumed her devious ways, and the next time she was in town, she went directly to the coach house to see if the ticket she held had any monetary value.

"Yes, the ticket is valid," the agent at the counter told her. "I made the schedule for Miss Cathy Willis's travels myself. Mrs. Willis didn't know exactly what date the trip would take place, so we left it open ended. It has been quite awhile ago now. Let's see—"

"How much did she pay for the ticket, Mr. Stroud?"

The man looked over his pince-nez. "Not knowing how much luggage the girl would need to take, Mrs. Willis put up a ten-dollar deposit, Mrs. Gomer."

"Ten dollars!"

"Not that it should matter to anyone. The woman painted many hours by lamplight to earn the extra money for the ticket. She was quite an artist! I displayed some of her work right here, and it was snapped up by traveling businessmen. I sometimes wonder if the long hours of painting didn't contribute to the breakdown of her health. Or perhaps she knew that she was failing and wanted the girl to have the trip—"

"You see, Mr. Stroud, Catherine Willis owed me some money when she passed on. Cathy said that I should have the coach ticket to be applied to the delinquent payment. She didn't care to make the trip anyhow; she wished to stay here with her friends."

"*You* are going to make the trip instead, Mrs. Gomer?"

"Oh, no, no! I couldn't leave poor Percival. He is as helpless as a baby when it comes to doing for himself! Cathy said she was sure that you would refund the purchase price of the ticket."

Mr. Stroud pinioned her to the wall with his scrutiny, staunching her glib flow of words. The whole population of Roby knew of Ruth Gomer's selfish ways and disapproved of them. Suspicion now narrowed the agent's eyes.

"I'm sorry, Mrs. Gomer, but this was a nonrefundable ticket. I made that quite clear to Catherine Willis when she paid cash for it. We are a business, and we can't maintain a profitable operation by giving people's money *back* to them."

"But in this case—in the case of death—" Ruth was persistent, an ugly greed pressing her on.

"In the case of death, Catherine Willis no longer has any needs. But I'll wager the young lady *does*. Upon the death of Mrs. Willis, the ticket became the girl's legal property. For you to be in possession of another's property could put you in great jeopardy if I should press charges against you—"

"But . . . but certainly you wouldn't do that since it was an honest . . . er, a mistake on my part to accept the ticket as payment of a debt! How could I have known it was against the law?"

Mr. Stroud knew where to hit and how to turn up the fire. He seemed to enjoy the game. "I will not turn you over to the authorities under one condition, Mrs. Gomer."

"I will gladly comply, Mr. Stroud. Truly I will. It was an honest, er, that is, an error on the part of both of us. Cathy wouldn't have *given* it to me had she known that transferring it was a crime. She's just a girl; she didn't know. What should I do to make amends?"

"Perhaps I should talk to the girl myself."

"I . . . I don't think that will be necessary. Can't we work this out between us?"

"Perhaps, but you must return the ticket to the proper owner immediately. Is she staying with you?"

"Er . . . no, she is visiting, ah . . . some friends. But I will see that she gets it."

"How soon?"

"Uh . . . today." She glanced uneasily at the grandfather clock on the wall, and as if on cue, it struck four o'clock. "It's a piece to the . . . the friend's house. It might be . . . tomorrow."

"No later than tomorrow, Mrs. Gomer. I will hold off the indictment until tomorrow afternoon. You have twenty-four hours." His look bored into the brooch on her coat. "*Any property* that belonged to a deceased person is passed to the living heirs. If *anything* is found in the possession of another without written evidence—"

Ruth's hand flew to cover the brooch. "All the . . . the

35

furniture was burned when lightning struck the house where Catherine lived."

"Just be sure to get *everything* straightened out, Mrs. Gomer. No later than tomorrow." His eyes were still glued to the spot where her hand covered the emerald.

"Yes, sir."

At home, Ruth fretted to her husband that Catherine Willis had put up *ten dollars* on a coach ticket for Cathy to go to Lord-knows-where. "Mr. Stroud said she painted for the money. If she painted for a coach ticket, she could have painted to pay higher rent."

"I'm sure her rent was sufficient, Ruth."

"And that skinflint, Mr. Stroud, wouldn't give me any money back on the ticket!"

"Well, Ruth, I'm sure he didn't want to make you an object of charity and take away your human dignity," Percival said. "At least *he* understands women even if I don't. I'm sure that the more it *cost* you to provide a place for Mrs. Willis and the girl, the more *self-worth* you feel." He paused. "And I've been thinking, Ruth. What you've said makes sense. You have such a generous heart and perceptive mind that you just might be ready if Gabriel blows his horn today."

CHAPTER FIVE

Deliverance

Problems sprouted like broom weeds for Cathy. As soon as she chopped one down, two grew in its place. She admonished herself to expect anything, to be surprised at nothing. Yet when Miss Weems flogged her with the awful accusation that morning, the injustice of it left her bankrupt.

As she donned her faded apron to begin work, the frowning matron accosted her. "Cathy Willis!"

"It is Dillingham, ma'am."

"Neither you nor I have reason to change your name, Miss Willis."

"My grandmother—"

"How fortunate that your grandmother didn't live to see your degradation! I would not have judged you to be such a *tramp*, but I've learned I can be fooled. I dared hope that you would be different from the other virtueless girls I have had in the past. But, no! You flirt and scheme and throw yourself at the boss's son like a . . . a . . . a well, I won't call you what the Bible does!"

Cathy felt an angry rush of blood rising to her neck and rushing toward her ears. "I beg your pardon, Miss Weems?"

"Blushing, eh? I'm surprised that one so brash has that ability. One who takes the beautiful womanhood given by God and desecrates it with *seduction!*"

"Miss Weems!" Cathy whirled about and faced the woman, heedless of the repercussions her fury might bring. "That is quite enough! *I don't even know what you are talking about!*"

"Go ahead and strike me!" taunted the matron. "And make me react. Then you can tell Keeper Bates, and he can tell his father, and—"

"Miss Weems, please. You are not reasonable; you are beside yourself. I care nothing for the boss's son or any other young man."

"Oh, so now you presume to add lying to your sins."

"The truth will speak for itself."

"Indeed it will. Indeed it *has.* Think of that while you're flitting about in the canyon today."

"In the canyon?"

"On your picnic."

"I know nothing of a picnic."

"You can present a most innocent countenance, Cathy."

"I'd be glad to know more about the picnic."

"Very well, I shall tell you. You've gone out of your way to curry favor of a young man. I saw you conversing with him in the kitchen. No need to deny it."

"I told him to go away."

She gave a sarcastic laugh. "He's going all right, and taking you with him. He has arranged that the two of you wile away half a day on an idle romp when a decent girl would be working."

"Are you speaking of Keeper?"

"None other, Miss Willis."

"I shall not go."

"Oh, but you shall go. Whatever Keeper Bates sets his head to, no one may withhold from him. He is a *spoiled heathen*. And let me tell you, young lady, to him you are nothing but a passing fancy. He will besmirch your name, drop you, and leave you with a mangled heart *and* a tainted future. Harvest time comes for all evil deeds."

"But Miss Weems, I don't wish to be in the company of Keeper . . . alone. You must believe me. Truly, I don't!"

"Well, *I* certainly won't accompany you, Cathy."

"I had rather die than . . . go with him."

"You'd best die abruptly then. It is my orders to prepare a picnic basket with enough supplies to feed the home for a week, and he will come for you at two o'clock. Nobody around here disobeys orders from any member of the boss's family. That would be suicide."

Cathy's hands trembled as she dipped up the breakfast mush. A pallor overspread her face when she thought of the prospects of an afternoon with Keeper. She had as soon meet a poisonous viper in the canyon as Keeper Bates. The venom of a serpent could only destroy the body, but an unprincipled man could kill one's honor and reputation.

At first, the hours passed slowly, then time accelerated. Faster. And yet faster. Then with his black boots spit-shined and his hair tamed with axle grease, Keeper came to the kitchen for her. He looked more menacing than ever in his fried shirt.

"You need some fresh air, dolly," he said carelessly. "You are looking peaked. I told the old bag to start feeding you better, but I see she can't be trusted. I'll start seeing after you myself. You'll be out of the kitchen soon. This little outing today is a trial run to see if you're fit for a Keeper. I've already warned Pa that when I find the one I want, I'll keep 'er."

He gripped Cathy's arm with a hamlike hand, swinging the basket in the other. The path he took led away to the thick shinnery behind the big house. "Women are looking out every window! You're the envy of them all today."

Icy fingers of dread tore at Cathy's throat, choking off her breath. Her mind, as well as her eyes, darted this way and that for an escape. She decided she would break and run when she got into the canyon. Keeper was much stronger than she, but being overweight he was probably slow on his feet. She would run away, throwing herself on the mercies of the wilderness, even if she met her fate by starvation or wild beasts.

"Don't be so skittish, dolly." Keeper smiled his slyest, reminding Cathy of Satan. "Most girls like to go for a lark. It beats the humdrum of work. You're not very tame, are you? Ah, but I can fix that. I've tamed many a kitten before. It's a great hobby of mine."

Cathy watched for her chance, and when Keeper relaxed his grip on her, she sprinted away like the wind. But with one giant pounce, Keeper clamped his hand on her shoulder in a vicious clasp. "Not so quick there. When Keeper has plans for a girl, he plans to keep 'er. There's no call for you to be such a wild thing anyhow. I see that I must start to domesticate you right away. And I don't spend my energy on just any idle project. Very likely, you'll be worth my time."

"I . . . I don't like you."

Mockery and scorn met in Keeper's smoldering glare. "But I like *you,* dolly, and that's what matters. I might even marry you when I get you conquered."

"I'll *never* marry you!"

"There you go fighting. Oh, but I like it! With your back arched and hissing like a barnyard cat at a stick, you're *cute.* And you don't know that you're spitting at the hand that will feed you—and feed you well. Actually, I can do you a lot of favors."

"I don't want favors."

"But I do."

The sun shone through the squatty scrub oaks, bringing warmth to the earth's cold cheeks but doing nothing to unthaw the hoary frost of hopelessness that locked Cathy in its arctic grasp. The footpath led them farther and farther away from the house and closer to the canyon. *Please God, help me* . . . The words seemed more like a dying plea than a prayer.

They came to an opening that led to a natural cave. Keeper demanded that Cathy spread their lunch on the cavern floor. It was a wonderful feast, complete with a lovely sponge cake, but Cathy tasted none of it; it stuck in her throat.

"Now, come and sit near me," invited Keeper when he had finished eating. He patted the ground beside him. "I have some secrets to whisper in your ear."

Cathy didn't move.

"Stuck to the sod, huh? Then I'll come to you." A glassy wildness danced in his eyes. He moved his face close to hers and reached for her single braid of hair.

"No!" she screamed, trying to push him away but finding it useless.

Keeper's leering laugh had hardly left his lips when a man bounded through the mouth of the cave. "Mr. Keeper, your father sent me to find you and the lady. He says that Miss Willis is needed at the house at once. Some emergency."

"How did you find us?" seethed Keeper.

"As simple as following your tracks in the sand."

"I'll bring her when I'm good and ready. Tell the old man we're having fun."

"No, sir. Mr. Bates instructed me to bring the lady back with me. And that I shall do. My job depends on it." He turned to Cathy, ignoring Keeper's loud protests. "Come, miss."

Keeper showed his blind fury by spewing oaths into the clean air. "Of all days, why today? Pa knew I had a picnic planned!"

"Orders, Mr. Keeper." Cathy's deliverer took her by the hand and pulled her to her feet. "I hope you're not too disappointed, miss." The look of pure gratitude that she gave him needed no interpretation.

"There'll be another time." Keeper glared at Cathy. "And that's a *promise.*"

When Cathy reached the farm, she was ushered into Mr. Bates's office, where Ruth Gomer sat twisting a handkerchief into knots. "Please be seated, Miss Willis." Mr. Bates nodded toward a chair. "Mrs. Gomer has asked to speak to you on a most urgent matter."

Ruth's eyes sought out various objects in the room but evaded Cathy. "I, uh . . . I'm sorry to disturb your delightful afternoon, Cathy. Mr. Bates assured me that you are adjusting well and are quite content here. The news I bring may not be welcome. That is . . ." Some distraction short-circuited her concentration. "I'll start at the first. Lightning struck the house where you lived with your grandmother and everything was lost."

"The paintings and the quilts?"

"*I* lost everything."

"So you need the quilt that I have?" supplied Cathy in an effort to forecast Mrs. Gomer's motive for coming.

"Oh, no, no, dear! In fact, Percy insisted that we absorb all the funeral expenses ourselves. He felt that I should . . . that I should return your coach ticket, as well as the emerald brooch, so that you may leave the farm *if you wish*. Mr. Bates tells me that likely you will not wish to do so now that you have become so fond of his son—"

"I do wish to leave, Mrs. Gomer."

"I took it upon myself to check and make sure the ticket is still current, and the agent at the coach house assured me that it is. Catherine put up a ten-dollar deposit for your trip and for the luggage."

"Where will you be going?" interrupted Mr. Bates, his florid face becoming even more flushed.

"To my father. My name isn't really Willis. It's Dillingham. My father is Ed Dillingham."

Mr. Bates started. *"Ed Dillingham?"*

"Do you know him, Mr. Bates?" questioned Mrs. Gomer.

"No. Well, that is, I do know of an Ed Dillingham, but he couldn't possibly be one and the same. He lives a great distance from here, and he hadn't a daughter, only a son."

Obviously displeased at the turn of events, Mr. Bates looked toward the door, changing his grimace to a smile as someone passed. He nodded to the passerby before turning his attention back to Cathy.

"Then I . . . I can go to my father?" At that moment, Cathy's joy was only surpassed by her surprise.

"Through my generosity, yes," Ruth emphasized. "Here is Catherine's purse with the ticket and brooch inside." She dropped the handbag into Cathy's lap as if it were a thing aflame.

"And if you will gather your things and put them in the wagon while Mrs. Gomer and I finish our business, she will take you to the station," Mr. Bates said.

A stiff-lipped Miss Weems helped Cathy fold her garments. "Mr. Bates said that you are to have what you brought," she said coldly. "I was obliged to run your dresses off the backs of two women. And here's your quilt—"

"I'd like for little Bonny to have the quilt, please, Miss Weems. She'll be cold at night without it."

"Just so Mr. Bates knows that it wasn't *my* idea to keep your quilt for the child. And you'll please not mention our conversation in the kitchen this morning to Mr. Bates."

"You do your job of seeing that Bonny gets the quilt and I'll conform to your wishes."

With a singing heart, Cathy ran to the wagon and placed her belongings beneath the seat. She then returned to the office to advise Ruth that she was ready.

"We hate to lose you, Miss Willis," Mr. Bates said. "Keeper has so few friends that it always cheers my heart when he finds someone with whom he can get along."

"I'm sure he will find someone more his *type*, Mr. Bates." So saying, Cathy swept from the room.

Ruth Gomer treated Cathy queenly on the way to town. "Mr. Stroud might take it in his head to ask you some strange questions about the coach ticket, Cathy," she said. "Don't give him any unnecessary information. It could interfere with your trip, or at least delay it. He is a most forgetful man. Doubtless, he will forget what I told him or get it all mixed together with someone else's problems. All that matters is that the ticket is good."

"Yes, that's all that matters. When I am settled with my father, I will work and send the money for grandmother's funeral. If I may have the undertaker's address—"

"Oh, no, no! Percy and I will take care of that."

"But I'd rather—"

"Now please don't say another word about it, my dear girl. It is enough to know that you were not mistreated on the poor farm and that you liked it there. I worried myself sick about you; I couldn't sleep a wink at night. Then when I learned that the ticket was authentic and not a figment of Catherine's disoriented mind, I was so overjoyed that I couldn't wait to get it to you! I actually cried from relief!"

However, when they arrived at the stagecoach station, the purse that held Cathy's ticket was nowhere to be found.

CHAPTER SIX

The Dilemma

"Where could the ticket be, Cathy?" Mrs. Gomer's voice carried an edge. "Are you sure that you put the purse in the wagon?"

"I'm most certain that I did, Mrs. Gomer. I put it right here under the seat on my side."

"Oh, the carelessness of youth!" fumed Ruth. "I should have seen to the ticket myself!" She felt under the seat and looked about the floorboard. "It couldn't have walked off!"

Tears budded behind Cathy's eyes. "Now what shall I do?"

"If we can't find it, Cathy, you will have no choice but to return to the poorhouse. However, since you were so content there, that shouldn't cause you any great distress—"

"I wasn't content there, Mrs. Gomer. I hated it!"

"Now, now. Mr. Bates said you were happy there; he should know. You are only angry and disappointed because the adventures of the trip have been lost. All children like excitement. That's part of the fickleness of youth. Those mood swings! I can still remember when I was your age and how changeable my emotions were. Big things seemed small and small things seemed big. An adolescent has no idea what is truly important in life. Why, you could marry Mr. Bates's son and be *rich*—"

"Will you take me back along the road to search for the ticket, Mrs. Gomer? Perhaps the purse dropped out along the way."

"Under other circumstances, I wouldn't bother. But Mr. Stroud was insistent that you have that ticket. I'll do it for *him*. However, it is too late to return today. You'll stay with me tonight, and we'll go first thing in the morning. I'll send Percy with a note to Mr. Stroud explaining that we need an extension of time."

"The ticket doesn't *expire* today, does it?"

"No, but—"

"Then it shouldn't matter to Mr. Stroud what happened to the ticket. He got his money."

"But I think it will be best to notify the agent that we need one more day."

"For what? I'm afraid I don't understand."

"Just forget it."

Linoleum covered floors and papered walls made Ruth Gomer's house a veritable heaven in comparison to the accommodations Cathy had known. Embroidered scarves and crocheted doilies created by the hands of her grandmother covered every bare surface. Cathy recognized them, and the memories brought a pang. *Grandmother did all this to provide for me*, Cathy told herself, *but to what avail if I come to an infamous end?*

The feather mattress that embraced Cathy's emaciated body provided glorious comfort, and she could have slept comfortably had she not been plagued with the tormenting fear of returning to the poorhouse. And even that she could tolerate, she allowed, if it were not for the wicked Keeper Bates.

Fragments of conversation from the Gomer's bedroom seeped through the wall. "No, Percy . . . won't keep her . . . will adjust again . . . Mr. Bates said . . . happy . . . his son . . . her own fault about the ticket." Mrs. Gomer was relegating her back to the farm. She put her hands over her ears to keep from hearing more.

The following morning, they retraced their route to the poorhouse. Cathy strained her eyes in an effort to cover the landscape on all sides and before them in hopes of sighting the purse. *I must find it,* her heart pounded. *Please help me, God!* But she did not find it.

At the farm, she went directly to Mr. Bates's office, hoping that she would not meet Keeper. Mr. Bates's office was locked, and Miss Weems said that he and Keeper had gone to the city for supplies. And no, she hadn't seen Cathy's lost purse, nor had she heard anyone mention finding it. And yes, if it was turned in, she would direct it to Mr. Bates.

Cathy returned to the wagon, a heaviness gathering around her heart. "It isn't here," she told Ruth Gomer.

"Then you will have no choice but to reside at the farm again, Cathy," Ruth said. "But like I told Percy last night, it will probably be the best thing for you. You are young and will adjust nicely this time just as you did the first time—only more quickly. Now you have a friend!"

Cathy turned to walk away, feeling faint and dizzy. Hope no longer whispered to her of a future.

"Wait! Where are you going?"

"Now that I'm here, I'll just stay and save you a trip."

"You must go back to town with me to talk with Mr. Stroud and tell him what happened! Tell him I brought your ticket to you and you lost it and that it was no fault of mine."

"You can tell him."

"No, *you* must tell him. That's the . . . the rule on lost tickets. Get in quickly and I'll take you back to town so that we may be done with it." Ruth grew agitated. "I certainly didn't know that this was going to cause me so much trouble! This is the third trip I've made!"

Cathy stood rooted in her tracks as white as a marble mantle. "I will not put you out another minute, Mrs. Gomer. Please accept my apologies for the trouble I have caused you already. Do whatever you wish about Mr. Stroud and the ticket." She darted through the gate and into the poorhouse.

"Oh, dear, dear!" muttered Ruth Gomer, hurriedly climbing down from the wagon to follow the fleeing girl. "Look what I have done now! Cathy! Cathy!"

There was no answer.

She wedged her oversized body through the gate and then the front door, chuffing along the corridor until she found Cathy. "You *will* come with me to Mr. Stroud and get this quagmire straightened out, Cathy Dillingham!"

"There's nothing to straighten out, Mrs. Gomer. The ticket is lost, I am forever doomed to the poor farm—and that's that." Her voice was flat.

"But . . . but we forgot your extra clothes, and I had a . . . a pillowcase for you that your grandmother smocked. Besides, Percy rather enjoyed your company, and he'll be glad for you to stay one more night."

"No, thanks. It will only make returning here tomorrow the harder."

"Then you can stay with us for a week."

"That would solve nothing."

"Please, Cathy, don't be contrary," she wheedled. "What must I pay you to go with me to Mr. Stroud?"

"Pay me?"

"If you *must know*, Mr. Stroud said he would hold me responsible for the ticket until he talked to you in person. I don't have the money to replace it and it . . . it could go very badly for me if you don't come along. The trips have been no trouble at all, really. I don't know what made me say they were. You can only cause me problems if you *don't* come with me. Now come along like a good girl. I'll buy you a soda at the drugstore."

Cathy, now thoroughly confused and weary, returned to the wagon. She was silent and withdrawn all the way to town, feeling that life had tossed her about until she was battered and spent, too tired to try to get a prayer past the demons of doubt.

At the coach house, she went in with Ruth Gomer and sat mutely while Ruth explained to the impervious Mr. Stroud that Cathy had carelessly lost the ticket her grandmother had purchased for her.

"Is that correct, Miss Willis?" prodded Mr. Stroud. "Am I to understand that Mrs. Gomer returned the ticket to you and then you misplaced it?"

"Yes, sir."

"Did she return any other property to you?"

Ruth shook her head, trying to catch Cathy's eye, but it was too late. "Yes, sir. She returned my grandmother's purse and a brooch. But I lost them, too."

"Does she now have anything that belongs to you?"

"No, sir. Everything else that my grandmother possessed was burned in the cabin fire."

"Mrs. Gomer owes you nothing?"

"Nothing, sir."

"Very well, then. The lost ticket will be no problem at all. I am the one who issued it, and I can furnish a replacement as easily."

Cathy's eyes glistened with glad tears. "You can? I can still make the trip?"

"Most certainly. When would you like to depart?"

"Oh, as soon as possible, sir!"

"On the next outgoing coach?"

"Oh, yes, sir!"

"The stage will come through in three days—"

Cathy's face fell. "That would mean yet another trip out to the poor farm for Mrs. Gomer."

"The poor farm?"

"Yes, sir. That's where I have been living."

All of Ruth's facial expressions and frantic gestures were lost on Cathy.

"Do you have friends with whom you lived there, Miss Willis?"

"No, sir."

"You mean you gave Ruth Gomer that expensive emerald and admitted yourself to the *poor farm?*"

"I didn't—"

Ruth cleared her throat loudly. "Please, Mr. Stroud! Let's let bygones be bygones. To talk about Cathy's grandmother brings her considerable anguish. Let me assure you that Cathy will not have to wait for the coach at the poorhouse. Percival and I will be *delighted* to see to her needs *in a most gracious manner* until time for her to depart."

"Is that agreeable, Miss Willis?" The proprietor looked directly into Cathy's eyes.

"Yes, sir."

"Then I shall keep your ticket here so that there will be no chance of it being lost or taken."

He looked at Ruth, who sputtered, "*I* didn't take her ticket, Mr. Stroud! I'd have no use for it!"

"And I hope, Miss Willis, that you will have a most pleasant trip."

He dismissed them with a curt nod.

CHAPTER SEVEN

Keeper's Plan

Keeper Bates sported a devilish grin. He'd watched Cathy place the old black purse under the wagon seat. When she returned to the building for Mrs. Gomer, he took it. Eavesdropping outside the door of his father's office apprised him of Cathy's ticket in the handbag. Without it, she would go nowhere. In a matter of hours, she would be back to the poor farm, back into his grasp. Ah, Keeper would keep 'er, all right! She wouldn't get away that easily!

That same day, his father invited him to go to Abilene on a supply mission. His doting parent, thinking him melancholy, was making restitution for the interrupted picnic. Keeper liked the advantages of his father's methods of apology. Of course, Mr. Bates didn't know about the purse or the ticket, but he wouldn't reprimand Keeper if he did. One so given to dishonesty himself could hardly censure dishonesty in another.

"My girl will be back by the time we return," Keeper told his father.

"She seemed excited to be going to her father."

"She'll change her mind and come back to me."

The city, with its exciting sights and smells, enraptured Keeper. He was especially fond of the square where vendors displayed their wares. Arrays of locally made food and merchandise lined the boardwalks: woven baskets, harnesses, milking stools, sacks of pipe tobacco, and bric-a-brac. Everywhere men were calling, laughing, jesting, the heels of their boots striking music on the planks of the walkway. The spirit of it made Keeper's heart race.

However, what he liked best was the smoky-windowed tavern, trimmed with gaudy lattice work that caught the reflection of sunset, throwing back the sunlight while blotting out the evil brewing within. He passed considerable time in the taproom watching the saloon girls. A shameful share of the "government money" went to strong drink.

He partook of all the town's perversity, but nothing could hold Keeper's attention for long. When the wait for the supply wagon stretched from a day to a week, he became restless and irritable. Mr. Bates found that it took more and more money to keep his son pacified—which left less and less for staples for the farm's occupants. The already weak porridges would have to be watered down yet more. If the supply wagon didn't come soon, he would be obliged to go home empty-handed!

"If that grub doesn't come in tomorrow, I'll just *walk* home," thundered Keeper, his patience gone awry.

"Why the rush, son? At least life is less tedious here than there. There are places of entertainment all around us."

"She'll be back by now."

"She . . . who?"

"Cathy."

"She'll be on the coach and gone."

He snorted. "She'll be there. You'll see!"

"Why, Keeper, I believe that you are in love! But then, you're old enough. I was married twice by the time I was your age. I don't know but that it would be a good thing for you. I suppose you'll not be satisfied until you have a woman to call your own." He sighed. "Few women can abide a bottle-bibbing man."

When they returned to the farm, however, Cathy was not there. With mounting agitation, Keeper confronted Miss Weems. "Where is Cathy?"

"I don't know, Mr. Keeper."

"Has she been back?"

"Yes, she came back looking for her purse. She had lost it. But nobody here had seen it."

"So she left again?"

"Yes."

"Say 'Yes, *sir*' to me!"

"Yes, *sir.*"

"And she hasn't returned."

"No . . . *sir.*"

When Cathy didn't show up at the poorhouse, Keeper went to Roby looking for her. He went directly to Ruth Gomer's house.

"What are you doing here?" Ruth Gomer asked, opening the door but a crack. "I made a deal with your pa— and I'm working on it!"

"I'm not here for Pa's business; I'm here for *my* business."

The door opened a bit more. "And what do you want of me?"

"I want to speak to Cathy."

"You found her purse?"

"Yes, I did."

"It's too late. She left three days ago."

"Where did she go?"

"She went to her father."

"She took off *walking*?"

"No, she went by coach—"

"Without a ticket? Her ticket is in this purse."

"Mr. Stroud issued her another one in place of the one she'd lost."

Keeper, unaccustomed to being thwarted, became livid at the thought that Cathy had escaped him. Revenge and desire worked together to form a plan to find her and make her pay "to the last farthing" for slipping from his clutch.

"You knew that she was in love with me and we'd planned to be married?"

"That's nothing to me." Ruth Gomer shut the door in the young man's face, incensing him the more. He removed the ticket and the brooch from the purse, dropped them into his pocket, and flung the handbag at the closed door.

It hit with a bang, and when Percival opened the door, Keeper ran, revealing his cowardice.

Now what? The ticket! He had a ticket. It was valid, and it would take him to her. He'd worry about getting them both back later.

At the stage station, he sat down on the backless bench to await his turn at the counter. The more the impromptu plan unraveled in his mind, the broader his smirk. He'd come back married! Then if he found he didn't like his bride, he'd simply discard her.

"You're going west, madam?" the attendant asked a customer.

"No, sir. I'm going east."

"Today's coach is westbound. You are holding an eastbound voucher. Eastbound tickets are blue; westbound are red. The coach you need will be through Friday afternoon."

Ah, now he knew! Keeper held a blue ticket. She had gone east, and come Friday, he would be on her trail. He got up and slipped out the door.

Mr. Stroud frowned. "Was that young man with you, madam?"

"No, sir. I've never seen him before."

"He left out in a mighty smoke. I didn't like his looks; he had shifty eyes. Up to no good, I'd venture."

Back at the farm, Keeper made life miserable for everyone. He kicked the animals, swore at the cook, and showed excessive rudeness to the residents. When he announced on Friday morning that he would be gone for a few days, everybody—including his father—breathed a sigh of relief. "Just don't get in trouble with the law, Keeper!" warned his father. "I don't want to waste my money on a lawyer."

At the stage stop, Keeper handed his ticket to the driver and started to climb aboard. "Ho, there, young man!" the driver called. "This ticket must be stamped by the man inside. And hurry it up. We're ready to pull out."

Keeper dashed into the depot and shoved his ticket toward Mr. Stroud, who recognized him from earlier in the week. "Stamp it," demanded Keeper. "And be quick about it!"

Mr. Stroud looked at the ticket then hesitated. "This ticket . . . you bought it here?"

"A friend bought it for me. But it's paid for, so why the fuss?"

"I need to do a bit of investigating on this particular ticket, sir."

"What's the matter?" yelled Keeper, losing his temper. "It's a perfectly good ticket, and the coach is leaving! It is imperative that I be on this coach! Stamp it and let me go!"

"Unfortunately, young man, I can't do that. I issued this ticket myself—to a Catherine Willis. My pen was running out of ink, and I traced over some of the numbers. See here?"

"Why does it matter who uses it? It's a good ticket, isn't it?"

"I can refuse to stamp it."

"You can't. It's discrimination."

"I can. I reissued this same ticket to Miss Cathy Willis a week ago. This ticket was lost—or it was stolen."

"Stolen?" Keeper threw back his head and laughed roguishly. "Who would steal a ticket?"

"Therefore," said Mr. Stroud, "I must invalidate this one." He reached for the ticket on the counter, but Keeper's hand was quicker.

"I'll keep it for a keepsake *just as it is.*" Keeper stalked from the room as the coach rumbled around the corner out of sight, headed east.

CHAPTER EIGHT

Mabel

Ed Dillingham bent over Lia's over-grown and sunken grave. Fifteen times the snows of winter had fallen on it, and the pain of her leaving was still raw. Would it ever go away?

For several months after Lia's death, Ed entertained the hope of finding his baby, little Edna. But when every lead proved futile, the shovel of discouragement dug the crypt for his dying hopes. He should have been more congenial with Catherine Willis, his piqued mother-in-law. He realized that now. Back then, the mantle of tolerance had not yet fallen upon his young shoulders.

Not a single day had he lived since Lia's death without the tormenting thoughts of Edna. The small face, too new to have distinction when he last saw it, had vanished from his memory. What would the child look like now? Would she favor Lia? Lia had been a beautiful woman, graceful of spirit and fair of face. Would Catherine tell the girl that she had a father? A brother?

Ed Dillingham's path in life seemed paved with mistakes. His initial mistake, he conceded, was calling for his mother-in-law when Lia lay at death's door. That error cost him his baby. His second mistake took him deeper into heartache. Before Lia's body turned to dust, a scheming widow with two small daughters moved in to claim his deceased wife's place. Blinded by grief, Ed married Mabel Norse before her true character emerged.

A proud and overbearing woman, Mabel insisted that Ed move to her home, a larger and more commodious facility. With the expanded family, they needed the extra room, she pointed out. This seemed reasonable to Ed, who was only too glad to remove himself from the surroundings which daily reminded him of Lia.

Immediately manipulating the affairs to suit her palate, Mabel insisted that Ed sell his place since the upkeep of two was both wearisome and unnecessary. On the surface, this too seemed a wise maneuver. Too late Ed woke up to the grim fact that Mabel now had all the property in her name. He had none. Nothing to pass on to his son, Edward. Nothing to offer Edna if he ever found her. Mabel's pampered girls would have everything. That had been Mabel's ambition and goal.

The lavish lifestyle that his second wife craved, Ed allowed, netted him a much more prosperous existence than he otherwise would have known. But he'd have chosen poverty with his peace-loving Lia a thousand times over the affluence with the luxury-hungry Mabel.

His new wife could refuse her own daughters nothing. They grew up to be spoiled, haughty, and self-willed. Neither was particularly pretty, and what beauty they might have had was diminished by their arrogance. All their friends were "bought."

Pearl was seventeen, Matilda sixteen. They showed little respect for Ed, appreciating nothing but the finance he could contribute to keep them in fancy attire. Mabel refused to let Ed correct them, instruct them, or guide them.

Ed was a praying man when he married Mabel. He still winced when he remembered the first time she caught him on his knees. "Whatever are you doing on the floor, Ed Dillingham?" she ridiculed. "Looking under the bed for monsters? Oh, but you look foolish! Do get up!"

He lifted his eyes to her scornful face. "Mabel, dear, I'm talking to my Father."

"To your *Father*?" She gave an irreverent hoot. "You've lost it, Eddie!" (He loathed the nickname and she knew it.)

"Yes, I've lost an awful lot, Mabel."

"Add your *mind* to the lot you've lost. Your father has been dead for twenty years! Putting your ear to the floor won't coax an answer from a corpse!"

"I'm not talking to a dead man, Mabel. I'm talking to God. And He's very much alive."

"Talking to *God*? Who do you think you are and what right have you to talk to Deity? He's busy turning the stars on at night and keeping the planets from self-destructing. He hasn't the time to listen to your paltry petitions. And if He had, He'd tell you that you're better off than half the world's population. Leave Him to help those who can't help themselves! Let Him help those poor wretches in my brother's poorhouse! What do *you* need anyway?"

"I need grace."

"Grace? Who is *she*?"

"Please be excused, Mabel, while I finish my praying. I consider it important even if you don't."

"You haven't time to idle away on such a trivial pastime, Ed. There's a thousand things to be done in the girls' room. As they grow older, they will need more clothes pegs and a shelf for their jewelry boxes. I need more pantry space myself. I didn't marry a man to have him shirk his responsibility by hiding under the cloak of prayer. A man who won't provide for his family is worse than an infidel. Prayers don't do infidels any good!"

Ed had never let Mabel catch him at prayer again, but he still asked for grace, for the return of his little daughter, and for a spirit free from bitterness. For these he made his request now as he knelt at Lia's headstone, the cold air whipping at his worn topcoat.

While thus kneeling, Ed prayed for his son, Edward. Now there was a boy to be proud of! Edward had emerged from beneath Mabel's rebuffs amazingly unscathed. Realizing he must make his own way in life, he had applied himself to learning all he could about everything he could. To further his education—and to escape the female domination at home—he had enrolled in Tarlton College in Stephenville early in the fall, working as a night watchman, never asking a penny's aid from anyone. He had rapidly advanced to the top of his class, winning many friends. One of these he planned to bring home with him for Christmas.

When Edward left for school, Mabel insisted that Matilda have his room. To this, Ed vigorously objected, causing Mabel to revert to one of her "sick headaches," a malady she contracted when she didn't get her way. Her nagging usually wore Ed down, but this time it didn't work. "Edward's room will be here exactly as he left it when he returns for the holidays!" Ed said, and he was unbending in his decision.

Some time after Ed's marriage to Mabel, he learned that her elder brother ran a poorhouse "out West." The man's wife had deserted him, leaving him with one son. Now he filled his coffers with the government subsidy meant for the occupants of the home and made a joke of it. Mabel thought him quite clever. Ed disagreed. He'd never met Mr. Bates, nor did he have a desire to do so. Any man who would oppress the poor was no man at all in Ed's books, and Ed would be quick to tell Tom Bates so. No, they wouldn't get along.

In her youth, Mabel had been pretty, but now at thirty-nine, all traces of her beauty were blotted out by her tyrannical disposition. She labeled her husband a monster of ingratitude if he crossed her. Wasn't it *her* house, *her* furniture, and *her* land that brought him his comfort?

Ed's constant grief for his absent daughter irked Mrs. Dillingham. Hadn't fate replaced the one of his with the two of hers? Why couldn't he be satisfied with Pearl and Matilda? She made no effort to help Ed in his search for Edna; she even hoped that she wouldn't have the burden of Ed's lost child. Edward, to whom she never bonded, was handful enough. Thank heavens, he had taken himself off to school now . . . and eventually she would have her way with his room. He could sleep on the divan when he came home!

Visiting the cemetery provided a touch of relief for Ed's sore heart, and he arose from his knees, brushing the dust from his trousers. He looked at the sky to determine how long he had been away and how long he dared stay yet. Blankets of clouds blocked out the winter sun; it looked like snow. He hoped the weather would hold until Edward could get in for the holidays.

Meanwhile, Mabel was at home reading the letter she had received from her brother, Tom Bates. He seldom took the time to write, but now and then he sent a note advising her of his growing fortune and his brilliant son, Keeper. These sanguine messages she shared with Pearl and Matilda but not with Ed. Ed had made some disparaging remarks about how Tom made his money.

In this letter, Tom made a passing mention of one of the poorhouse "varmints" named Cathy Willis who had gone in search of her father, one Ed Dillingham. Of course, the girl couldn't be the daughter of his brother-in-law, Mabel's husband. But it was an amusing coincidence. He described her as a "sprite little runt, fetching enough to turn Keeper's silly head." Mr. Bates stated that even though it meant a loss of income for him, he was rather glad she was gone since he wanted Keeper to make an "advantageous match" with the fringe benefits of wealth and property. But the boy *would* flirt now and then with the impoverished girls!

Mabel laughed aloud at the indigent girl's plagiary of Ed's name. It was a means of exodus for her, of course. She had probably found a scrap of an old letter with the Cranfills Gap address, or Keeper may have carelessly made mention of his Uncle Ed Dillingham (whom he had never seen). Poorhouse people would grasp at any straw, invent any fiction to escape their mean existence. The girl had probably eloped.

There was no reason to mention the incident to Ed. His child's name was Edna, not Cathy, and if this Cathy girl did find a way to contact Ed, it would be simple enough to prove her an impostor.

Mabel lifted the lid of the cook stove and fed the letter

to the hungry flames. It wouldn't do to give Ed a thread of hope. She had learned that he could take the smallest bit of yarn and turn it into an impossible tangle.

And a yarn this was.

CHAPTER NINE

The Journey

The storm blew in during the night. Roads, blocked by high drifts of snow, were wholly impassable. The stage on which Cathy journeyed had reached a place called Proctor's Inn, where she would turn south. Emergency lodging was provided for the stranded passengers, but Cathy was responsible for her own food.

She had but a dollar, placed in her hand by Percival Gomer (without Ruth's knowledge) as she departed the Roby station. For how long they might be stranded no one could predict. The dollar would have to stretch the entire breadth of the trip, and due to this extreme economy, Cathy had already so shorted herself on nourishment that her legs felt unstable beneath her.

The facility filled to capacity with the later arrival of a coach from the west. Smoke, voices, and smells mingled in the stuffy lodge. There were people everywhere and from all levels of society. Most of the passengers were men, and the few ladies who traveled the line were much older than Cathy.

Sorting them in her mind, Cathy put the men with frock coats and cigars in one pile and those with worn hats and boots in another. The ladies were all fashionably dressed, and Cathy knew that she presented a rather grotesque appearance in her spotted calico that was a year too short and in her black stockings that her grandmother had footed with white. She tried to stay out of notice, but the cramped quarters made it impossible to escape curious eyes.

Badgered by hunger, she sat at an oilcloth-covered booth eating a bowl of soup with half a loaf of bread that had cost her a frightening fifteen cents. She had come early to avoid the rush of customers who would soon be gathering for supper. Her soup, however, was so hot that precious time passed with its cooling, and to her chagrin, the cafe began to fill up. Patrons took other tables until there were no more vacant tables left to take.

The overcrowding brought two young men to her booth seeking a place to sit while they ate. "May we share your table?" asked one. "That is, if you haven't someone else coming."

Cathy would gladly have turned the table to them and fled, but she had paid an enormous price for her food, and she knew that she needed it lest she become faint before the next meal. In response to their question, she gave a bare nod then lowered her head quickly. But before she did, she noted that they were both clean-cut gentlemen, remarkably courteous and pleasing of countenance.

One had eyes the same color as her own. Looking at him was almost as if she were looking in a mirror. Intelligence mixed with the boyishness about him, and he had a firmness and decision that tattled of his inner strength. The other man was darker, more handsome, and probably older. She guessed them both to be nearly twenty years of age.

Cathy had no intentions of making conversation with them, but the brown-eyed one spoke up: "I suppose that we should introduce ourselves since we have been so rude as to disturb your meal, miss. I'm Edward and this is my friend, Davis."

Cathy kept her eyes on her bowl and said nothing.

"And I suppose your name must be a secret?" His eyes twinkled, and a quick glance told Cathy that he was teasing her.

"I'm . . . Cathy Willis." Years of habit produced the name her grandmother had given her, and she reddened when she remembered that she was now Cathy Dillingham. She had given the wrong name, but it was too late to change it now. Besides it didn't matter.

"Well, Cathy, whatever you've ordered smells delicious, and if you'll not think us copycats, we'll have some of the same."

"It . . . it is good." Her grandmother had warned her about conversing with strangers, but these young men seemed devoid of questionable motives. They were nothing at all like Keeper Bates. They were merely stuck in a snowstorm like herself.

"I suppose that you're going somewhere for the holidays?" The question came from Davis and was solicitous rather than prying.

"Yes. To my father's," Cathy answered.

"You can be thankful that you have a father," Davis said wistfully. "Mine went on to be with our Lord, and Edward has been so kind as to invite me to his home for Christmas. Else I'm afraid I would have to spend the season alone."

A great empathy for Davis arose in Cathy's bosom, and she gave him a rare smile, bringing to fore her uncommon beauty. He had mentioned the Lord, and that made her feel more at ease. Anyone who loved God couldn't be a threat to one's safety. "It's . . . it's bad to be alone," she said. "I know."

"Have you been traveling long?" asked Edward.

"For three days. I was with Ma . . . and . . . and . . ." Here Cathy's voice broke, but Edward rescued her by his smooth way of going on.

"Davis and I are roommates at school. Both of us are attending Tarlton State University. This is my first year and Davis's second. I'm taking elocution and he's studying to be a teacher. I'm used to girls; I have two stepsisters. But Davis isn't."

Cathy decided that Edward was teasing again, seeing that his revelation brought a deep blush to his friend's face.

"Nor am I used to . . . boys," Cathy admitted in Davis's defense so that he wouldn't feel alone.

"Where have you traveled from?"

"Roby. Out West."

"I've seen it on the map."

"It's just a small place."

"I don't know how long we'll be grounded here, Cathy, but eating by oneself is no fun. We'll be glad to take you under our wings and play big brothers to you since you've no traveling companion. We'll share your table at each meal, if you'd like," he lowered his voice. "It might be preferable to some of the less savory characters here."

"Thank you," Cathy said. "That would be nice." Arising to go, she made a small curtsy.

Back in her room, Cathy flung herself across the hard cot and cried. Cried from exhaustion. Cried from loneliness. And cried because she didn't have a brother like Edward. Then she cried because she was crying, and later because she didn't know why she was crying.

When the crying ceased, the questions started, and they were more draining to her emotions than the tears. What if there was no father to meet her at the end of the trip? If she really had a father, he could have moved away or died. Or—horror of horrors!—maybe he didn't want her! If he had not come for her in fifteen years, that was a great possibility. If he didn't want her, what right had she to intrude into his life now? And of all times, at Christmas time! That thought seemed the last drop in the brimming bucket of doubt. Many and bitter were the speculations that abused her overwrought mind as she lay wrestling with unknown demons and watching the daylight fade from the distant hills. She had been a fool to come!

Gradually her thoughts took on a definite purpose. She would not go to a place where she wasn't invited and might not be allowed to stay. She would ask the coach driver if she might return to Roby instead of going on. Yes, she would return. With that decision, she knew that she must not part with another cent more than she must spend to keep herself alive. She blocked out thoughts of the poorhouse, shut out all future miseries, and fell into a troubled sleep.

Edward had watched Cathy leave the dining room and shook his head. "Suffered a great deal, that one. Makes everything in you want to protect her, doesn't it?"

"How old would you guess her to be?"

"Probably older than she looks. Fifteen, maybe. And a very scared lass."

"You are a perceptive man, Edward."

"It comes of being around girls all my life. This girl is nothing like my sisters who have been pampered all their days. They are sixteen and seventeen."

"Will it cause them any inconvenience that I have come home with you?"

"Oh, no! They'll love it! They love all male attention! We'll have our own room to which we can resort if we tire of them. Pearl plays the pianola admirably and likes to show off her talent. And Matilda sings. There won't be a dull moment! You'll be glad to go back to school for a little solitude, I dare say!"

"Give me anything but solitude right now!"

Edward sobered. "I can't erase Cathy's face from my mind. I almost wish that we could take her home with us. It is obvious that she is acquainted with . . . with severe poverty."

"She didn't say which direction she was going from here, did she?"

"No, and I didn't press. She doesn't know us. When she learns that she can trust us, she will open up. She longs for companionship."

"You have a way with people, Edward Dillingham. You'd make a good parson."

"You must learn to observe, Davis," replied Edward. "You can learn a heap by simple observation."

CHAPTER TEN

Her Father's Name

Edward's observation served him well when Cathy had only a glass of milk for lunch the next day. He said nothing but kept up a comfortable chatter, telling her about his boyhood home, his dog Rambo, and his stepsisters, cracking jokes that brought a wan smile to her lips.

"Now my sister, Pearl, made a cake from a recipe she'd clipped from her mother's magazine. Everything went fine until the wind blew the recipe over. The other side told how to make a rock garden!"

Davis groaned. "Your humor is feeble today, Edward."

"I have one even better than that. My dog Rambo ate the first cake Matilda baked. I told her not to cry, I'd get another dog—"

"No more! No more!" Davis held up his hand. "Wait and let me meet these young cooks for myself. You're coloring my thinking!"

By suppertime, Edward's concern about Cathy had turned to anxiety. She ordered nothing but crackers and water. "Are you *very* homesick?" he asked the girl.

"N-no."

"You're not eating enough to keep a bird alive! Here.

I've ordered too much. Eat this cornbread." Color stained Cathy's face when he placed the bread in front to her, but she ate every bite of it.

"The girl is hungry," Edward told Davis later. "She's out of money. If we're beached much longer, she'll starve."

"I'll be glad to share my food with her," Davis offered rather quickly.

"But with caution," warned Edward. "She's an independent thing. If she gets the notion we're pitying her, she'll pull away from us."

Thereafter, one or the other of them "went overboard" with ordering and saw that Cathy had food from their own abundance. "I think she's getting wise to us," Edward said after a few such meals. "If we aren't careful, she'll balk on us—and go hungry again."

By the end of the week, the storm abated. The December sun, emerging from its hiding, looked out on the white, untrodden snow that covered the ground for miles around. Rapidly the roads were broken, and word circulated that the coaches would soon roll again.

Edward went to the lunchroom early, hoping for a last opportunity to talk with Cathy before the boarding call was given. He wanted to talk with her *alone*. Something like a bur clung to the lining of his mind in connection with the girl. Some gnawing memory, bleached by childhood forgetfulness, urged him to learn more of her plight.

When Cathy appeared, he motioned for her to join him at the table where he drank his black coffee. "The coaches are pulling out today. What is your final destination?" Her eyes were red-rimmed from crying. He held his breath for fear she wouldn't respond.

"I'm . . . I'm going back to Roby."

"Instead of going on to your father's for the holidays?"

"Yes, sir."

"Is it because you don't have the funds to go farther?"

"No, sir. That isn't the reason." She knotted her small hands together.

Something in her expression made Edward want to press on beyond his rights to do so. "Where had you started, Cathy? Where does your father live?"

"My destination was Cranfills Gap."

"*Cranfills Gap?*"

"Yes, sir. That's a funny name for a town, isn't it? I . . . I suppose that my father still lives there."

"He doesn't know that you are coming?"

"No, sir. I didn't know his address to write, and even if I had known, I didn't have a tablet or a stamp. I . . . I don't even know how I would find him if I got to Cranfills Gap. I . . . I should have thought of all this before I started—"

"I'm sure, Cathy, that your father will be very disappointed if you turn around and go back. Every father wants his children home for Christmas."

Great tears, as clear as diamonds, formed in the corners of Cathy's eyes. "If . . . if I could just know for sure that he . . . that he *wants* me!"

"Why wouldn't he?"

"Oh, I don't know, but he might have reasons. He hasn't seen me in . . . in so many years."

"Cathy, I know 'most everyone at Cranfills Gap. That's where I grew up, and in fact, that is where I am headed today. It's a small Norwegian community and very close-knit. It sits between two mountains, in the gap. Let's see, there's the Olafs and the Pedersons and the Orbecks and the Finsteds." He counted on his fingers:

"Bertelsens, Scheblers, Wieses, Rohnes, Carlins. Hmmmm . . . I can't find any Willises. I can't remember anyone ever living there by the name of *Willis*."

"Actually, Willis was my ma—that is, Grandma's name. I . . . I lived with her all my life until she passed away. My mother must have died when I was very small."

"And how old are you?"

"Nigh fifteen."

"And you don't even know your father's real name?"

"Yes, my grandmother told me his name as she was dying. She must have known that she wouldn't live long, for she bought me the ticket to go to him some time ago. I was at the poorhouse for a while and I . . . I lost the ticket, you see . . ." She covered her face with her hands. "Oh, I don't know why I'm telling you my troubles. Please forgive me."

"You must tell me everything, Cathy."

"No, I—"

"But *please*. You need an older head to help you make a very important decision just now, and I promise that I won't betray your trust. I have sisters of my own, and you can depend on me to act only in your best interest." His face was clear and honest.

"But why would you . . . care?"

"I do. Very much. So go on."

"When my grandmother died, everything she owned went to pay her back rent and the funeral expenses. The . . . the landlady took my ticket, and I had nowhere to go but to the poor farm. I hated it there—"

"To be sure."

"Then Mrs. Gomer—that's the landlady—brought my ticket back to me. But I . . . I lost it. I thought I would be forever doomed to the poor farm, but the station agent remembered issuing the original and he made me up another one.

"At first, I was very happy. But now I . . . I just don't know. You see, my father hasn't contacted me in all these many years. I know nothing of the circumstances of my birth. He may not even *want* me and I had rather die in the poorhouse than to be an embarrassment to him."

"Your grandmother left you with no money at all?"

"She had none. I had her emerald brooch, but I lost that, too. Mr. Gomer gave me a dollar—"

"A *dollar*?"

Cathy looked small and pitiful. "I've been trying to stretch it."

"You can't go back to Roby with less than a dollar!"

"But . . . I must."

"No, you mustn't." Edward's chin came up.

"What else shall I do?"

"You shall go home with *me* for the holidays."

"Oh, no! I couldn't impose upon a complete stranger!"

"I'm not a stranger. You've known me for almost a week. Have I tried to harm you?"

"No. But . . . but I just couldn't do that. Thank you, anyhow."

The invitation he had just offered, Edward knew, was ill-advised. Though his father would be delighted to have Cathy for the holidays, Mabel wouldn't. She would brook no rival for her own plain daughters, and Cathy's handsome face would set the girl at a disadvantage at once. Also, Pearl and Matilda would resent sharing their room. It was enough that he would ask them to entertain Davis, but being male and a novelty to his stepsisters, Davis would be treated well enough. With Cathy, it would be another story.

"Cathy, I can't let you return to the poorhouse. That's no place for a *lady* like you. We'll figure something—"

Here Davis put in his appearance. "Yes, we'll figure something," he grinned, showing even white teeth. "Now tell me what it is we're figuring, and I'll help with the math. Is it subtraction or division?"

"Cathy is apprehensive about completing her journey. She's threatening to backtrack. She's never met her father and—"

"Oh, I know just how you feel, Cathy!" Davis called her name with such feeling that Cathy felt a warm squeeze around her heart. She thought him one of the kindest young men she'd ever met. "I'm shy, too, and I have butterflies just thinking of meeting Edward's family, and I have Edward to break the ice for me."

"That's an idea!" Edward slapped his hands together.

"What's an idea?" Davis looked blank.

"We could go *with* Cathy to meet her father so she wouldn't be so nervous."

"Oh, no, no!" Cathy seemed more alarmed than ever. "Father would think me very 'fast' if I came along with two handsome men." Realizing what she had said, Cathy's cheeks dyed to a fiery red, making her the more lovely.

"We'll explain," promised Davis.

"Yes, we'll explain," rejoined Edward. "I can't place a Mr. Willis, but—"

"His name isn't Willis," Cathy reminded.

"I don't believe you ever told me your father's name."

"It's Dillingham. Ed Dillingham."

CHAPTER ELEVEN

No Room

Ed Dillingham picked up the vase just as he had done every day since he'd committed Lia's body to the earth. It was the only memoir to which he yet clung. Lia had bought it on their honeymoon, a drab clay pitcher with a small neck and handles on each side. She'd brought it home in her arms and painted on it, transforming it to a magnificent thing.

The pottery was an analogy of Lia's life. Everything she touched, be it ever so commonplace, was enriched by her sweet influence. The dark was made brighter, the earth more colorful by the stroke of her smile.

Mabel finally gave up in her efforts to dispose of the vessel. Ed prescribed such strict orders concerning it that she harbored a rare fear of his reaction should she disobey. When Ed's mind was determined, he could be a formidable force. She judged that if the place were on fire and he must choose between rescuing her or the vase, it would likely be the latter. He had a twisted sense of sentimentality.

"Papa-Ed's in there talking to that silly vase again, Mama," reported Matilda, rolling her eyes.

"What is he saying today?"

"He's saying, 'This belongs to you, little Edna.'" Her voice held a singsong mimic.

"Let him have his madness, Matilda. As long as he earns the bread, we can humor him in this one idiocy."

"I think that vase is the ugliest thing I've ever seen!" put in Pearl. *"Little Edna* can have it! I wish she'd come and get it. And the sooner the better!"

"After all these years," said Mabel, "we'll never see little Edna. I saw her when she was newborn, and that's all I ever care to see her. Now Pearl, you polish the silver. We're having a house guest."

"A house guest?"

"Yes. Edward is bringing someone from school. He wrote to Ed and asked permission."

"Heaven save us!" flared Matilda. "It's probably a bespeckled professor! Why do we get stuck with catering to *Edward's* friends?"

"It's his roommate."

"That could be worse!"

For all their complaining, the girls liked Edward; they'd missed him fiercely. He took much of the atmosphere's cheer with him when he left for college. Meals were silent affairs, evenings vapid without the sunshine of his disposition, his laughter, his charisma. They looked forward to his homecoming.

Ed passed through the kitchen. "I'll be gone for an hour or so," he said, heading for the back door.

"Stay all day if you wish," returned Mabel.

"Or all week!" Matilda said, looking after him. "Mama, I don't know why you ever married such a stick in the mud! You don't *match*. I do hope for a better counterpart for myself when I marry!"

"We benefited, Matilda. When you see a chance to move up, you do. This house was not nearly so comfortable before we enlarged and improved it with the money from Ed's place. And he does bring in an income from his timber cutting."

"Not nearly enough!" pouted Pearl. "When I am wed, it will be to a *rich* man. Papa-Ed will never get rich sawing lumber!"

"As for me," said Matilda, "I'm going to marry a *handsome* man. What is money compared to good looks? I want all my friends to drool with envy when I walk down the street."

"In rags?" taunted Pearl.

"Pretty is as pretty does, girls," interspersed Mabel.

"What day is Edward coming home, Mama?"

"Ed thought he would be here before now, but more than likely he has been delayed by the weather."

A sound caught Matilda's keen ear, and she ran to the window. "Oh, Pearl, come quickly! The stage has driven up to the gate, and I reckon Edward has come! Let's get a preview of our guest." She pushed aside the heavy curtains to see better.

From the mud-besplattered vehicle came a leg encased in a black stocking that turned to white near the bottom. Then the rest of the being was handed down by Edward.

"Oh, heaven help us!" shrieked Matilda. "It's *female*."

"If she's for here, she is not staying in our room for *one minute*, Matilda," Pearl's warning came along with squinted eyes for effect. "Mama!"

Mabel came as fast as her bulk would allow. "It's a girl and the very portrait of a beggar!" Pearl derided. "We're *not* permitting her to stay in *our* room with us. Is that understood?"

"I wouldn't think of allowing Ed's son to misput you, my dear. If he has brought a homeless waif home for *us* to care for, he can take her back where he found her. And promptly!"

Matilda spotted Davis. "And he's brought a gentleman, too. Ooooo! And *sooooooo* handsome!"

"And *sooooooo* rich," Pearl added. "Look at that London topcoat!"

"The girl could be the gentleman's sister."

"There's no connection! He's dressed to the nines, and the poor creature with them looks like a mangy polecat. Black and white hosiery! I hope she doesn't *smell* like a skunk, too!"

Edward collected their luggage from the boot of the coach. He handed a leather portmanteau down to Davis. "Ah, handsome," whispered Matilda. "That gorgeous hair . . ."

"Ah, rich," crooned Pearl. "A doeskin suitcase."

"But who's the girl?" wondered Mabel aloud, pulling the curtains open wider, forgetting that they could be seen peeping.

"Maybe she isn't getting off here. Maybe she just got off to stretch her legs before going on."

"Surely so," agreed Mabel. "I'd be ashamed for anyone to see her come to *my* front door. Indeed, she looks a fright."

But as they watched, the girl looked up into Edward's face with a trusting smile. He encircled her with his arm and led her toward the house.

"Disgusting!" spat Mabel. "What familiarity these colleges teach young folks nowadays!" With a jerking movement, she turned from the window and closed the drapes. "I'll have Ed speak with his son. The boy is *his* to handle, not mine. I'm not responsible for his decadence! *I* gave up on him long ago!" Then, smelling her cake burning, she made a fast waddle to the kitchen, still disgorging black thoughts.

Edward waved in the direction of the window where the stepsisters still tried to peek, causing them to jump back and drop the curtains. He entered without knocking, bringing along his companions. "I saw you two," he grinned. "A watched pot never boils! And *do* I have a surprise for you!"

Pearl and Matilda cast short, inquisitive glances at Davis to avoid an open stare. Which one would catch this fine specimen of manhood? They clothed their recent contempt in a robe of charming manners for his benefit.

"This is Davis, my roommate at school." Edward made the introduction calmly. "And this is my sister, Cathy. Where's Pa?"

"He went out. He'll be back in an hour or so."

Mabel stood in the kitchen doorway, nearly filling it. Her curiosity glued her feet to the floor. His *sister?* What warped sense of family extension had Edward picked up now? She'd heard that the doctrine of we're-all-brothers-and-sisters-in-this-human-race was being propagated. If this was the results of Edward's schooling, Ed must insist that his son come home at once! He must not be allowed to claim a kinship to such vagabonds so far below them on the social ladder. What would Mrs. Knudeson and the Jordensons say? She wouldn't have Edward laying *the Dillinghams* on the tongues of the neighbors! To expect

Pearl and Matilda to condescend to entertain a girl of low birth simply wasn't fair!

Yet when Cathy looked at Mabel, though her dress was outgrown and devoid of style, there was something in her fine features and open face that commanded respect. Cathy was not a girl to be looked upon and despised. Mabel felt it, and it awoke a bitter jealousy in her as she considered that if this girl were older and dressed properly, she might compete with her own daughters. She ground her teeth together when she saw that Cathy had a beauty quite aside from anyone she'd ever seen. It was as much a beauty of intellect as of face.

Whoever she is, she will never outdo my girls; I'll see to that. Mabel set her jaw and made a meager acknowledgment of Edward's introduction. *And I'll be rid of her as soon as Ed arrives! The Queen of England can sign her name to that!*

"I'll show Davis to our room, Cathy, so that he can get settled before dinner," Edward said to her with a special tenderness. "You may be seated there on the sofa until Pa gets back. It won't be long. I'll be right here for you if you need me."

Cathy took a seat but Mabel paced. Malicious thoughts turned cartwheels in Mabel's mind. *Yes, we'll see what Pa does when he gets home.* She wagged her head. *And how promptly!*

Matilda, though younger than Pearl, was the unofficial spokeswoman for her sister. Feeling it her duty to speak up now, she followed Edward to the door of his room and asked to have a word with him in private.

He gave a nod and waited for her to begin. "We're so pleased to have you home, Edward," she gushed. "*And* your roommate. We'll all have a wonderful holiday together, I'm sure."

"With Cathy here, it will be like no other!" exulted Edward.

"But we haven't room for the *girl*—"

"I figured that she could stay with you and Pearl until Davis and I go back to school. And then she can have my room."

"You're *leaving* her here?"

"Why, certainly! Pa will hear to nothing else!"

"I'm sorry, Edward, but you must send her back to . . . to wherever she lives."

"She lives right here. She has no other home."

"We simply cannot accommodate her. We're not an *orphanage.* If she must stay overnight, she will be obliged to sleep on the divan in the sitting room."

"Well, well, is there still no room in the inn?" Edward knew how to handle his stepsisters. "In that case, Davis and I will make arrangements to spend the night at a boardinghouse and give Cathy our room. Then tomorrow, we'll return to our dormitory at school."

"Oh, by no means, Edward!" The prospect of the male visitors taking their leave was a dreadful thing to Matilda. That would mean stale holidays, and Pearl would be infuriated! "We'll squeeze her in somehow, Edward—*just to please you!*"

The threat worked . . . just as Edward knew it would.

CHAPTER TWELVE

Reunion

Cathy's tired eyes siphoned splendor from the decorations around her. A cedar tree, decked with marvelous gewgaws and baubles, stood in one corner as if it grew there. Underneath the tree lay stacks and stacks of neatly wrapped packages.

She'd seen pictures of Christmas trees. She and Catherine had never had one; the high plains where they lived were lacking in evergreens. They'd put the prolific mistletoe over the door, but greenery purchased from a merchant was out of the question. Catherine had promised that "someday" they would have a "store-boughten tree," but the promise bogged down with all the other "someday" plans.

As a child, Cathy daydreamed of getting a book, a toy, or a vanity set for Christmas, but over the years, her gifts consisted of hand-knit items or horehound candy. Cathy never doubted her grandmother's noble intentions, and had she lived, perhaps they could have known a better life in the dim future.

Things would be different here at Cranfills Gap, though—and oh, so grand! There would be pretty dresses, good food, and lots of love. She'd have a *family*. Her emotions still whirled about like a dust devil on the prairie. They had not settled from the shock of finding that Edward Dillingham was her own brother. It had taken a while for her to absorb it.

When Edward first revealed his identity, she thought it might be an abduction trick. Edward *seemed* true, but what if he wasn't? Catherine hadn't mentioned a brother. Could it be that Catherine knew nothing about Edward? If she did know about him, why would she purposely withhold the information that would mean so much to Cathy? Cathy had seesawed between wanting to trust Edward and being afraid to let herself believe in him.

She closed her eyes to relive the last few miles of the trip to Cranfills Gap, the reviewing of which brought her feelings of rapture. As they traveled, Edward sat near her and told her everything he could remember of her beginning. It camped on the extreme fringes of his memory, he said, but it was there.

Mrs. Norse, the neighbor lady who later became his stepmother, cared for him when Cathy was born. He stayed with her in her home, the same house where they lived now. He recalled his mother, Lia, showing him the tiny bundle wrapped in pink blankets and saying it was his new sister. "You're to help Mommy protect and care for her, Edward," he quoted Lia as saying.

Then one morning when Mrs. Norse brought him back home, both his mother and the pink blanket were gone. His father walked the floor and cried, calling for his little Edna.

"Who was Edna?" asked Cathy.

"That was your birth name," Edward told her. "We

have your certificate of birth. You were named for Pa—and he was button-popping proud of you."

"Will I ever get used to being called Edna?"

"We'll call you Cathy if you'd rather."

"I'd rather. At least . . . at least for now. Otherwise, I might not remember who I am." She gave a crooked smile.

"Pa will be beside himself with joy. I'm not sure, but I think he has cried for you every day since you were . . . taken."

"Why did my grandmother take me away?"

"We're not sure. Lia was her only daughter, and she may have been trying to replace that daughter with you."

"Why didn't she take you, too?"

"Pa isn't sure that she even knew about me. Pa doesn't know how much Catherine and our mother communicated. There was some misunderstanding that caused a family rift, and Catherine never visited. Our mother may not have told Catherine about my birth. Only when she was at death's door did Pa send for her."

"What . . . what happened to my mother?"

"She fell and hit her head on the iron stove. I think you were about a week old when she died. Mabel—the former Mrs. Norse—brought me over once a day to see you and Ma."

"Then my grandmother left with me?"

"Yes. One night while Pa was asleep. We never heard from her again, though Pa asked everywhere he went. He never quit hoping . . ."

Edna. Catherine knew her name, of course, and that's why she'd had the "E" put on the handle of the spoon. And that's why she wouldn't answer Cathy's questions when she asked about the initial engraved there.

Fatigued from her surge of emotions and the stress of the trip, Cathy was soon asleep on the couch, her long fringed lashes resting on her white cheeks.

While Matilda talked with Edward, Pearl and her mother conversed in hushed tones in the kitchen. "Whatever shall we do with that *dreadful* creature, Mama?" Pearl implored. "What a faded and shapeless dress! And her shoes! Did you notice them? She can hardly keep them on, they're so large! They must have been handed down for *generations!* What shall we do if company comes? Polly Jermstad would have a laughing fit!"

"I've learned to endure what can't be helped. I'll see that it doesn't happen again. Edward hasn't the foresight of a headless chicken. If the girl must be here *temporarily,* I will try to keep her occupied and out of sight while you and Matilda enjoy that delightful gentleman named Davis. Isn't he just *too* easy on the eyes?"

Still Pearl sulked. "Will you try to convince Papa-Ed to talk his son into removing the nuisance *today?*"

"I'll try Pearl. Indeed, I will. But when it comes to Edward and his quirks, Ed is mush."

"But Mama, remember it is *our* house. It is *our* furniture. It is *our* land. You own it all. Haven't you a right to say who comes and who doesn't?"

"Put in those terms, I suppose I do."

"Then it's time to exercise your authority!" Pearl walked out, her head high.

Matilda joined Pearl in their room. "I'm afraid we'll have to take her in our room with us, Pearl."

"Never! *My* room will not be filled with a critter who might have lice! She might even be fitty, Matilda. Did you see how blue she is around the mouth?"

"Listen, Pearl. Edward has his stubborn head set. He says if we don't treat the girl top-notch, that he'll move out of his room and give it to *her*."

"What has bitten Edward?"

"Then, oh, get this: he will take Mr. Gorgeous and go right back to school!"

Pearl groaned. "He's got us! Whatever we have to do, we can't lose Mr. Rich. Christmas would be a drag without guys. Well, I wonder how much baggage the 'thing' will have to clutter up our room? I'm not giving up a clothes peg!"

"I didn't see any luggage at all."

Mabel heard her husband, Ed, at the back door and met him there. "Ed Dillingham, your son is home, but I need to speak with you before you go to greet him."

"Why, surely Mabel. But please make it snappy, for I'm most anxious to see my son. These four months that he's been away seem more like four years."

"He brought along an uninvited guest—"

"No, Mabel, he asked leave of me to bring his room-mate. I'm sure that I mentioned it to you and you were agreeable."

"I'm not talking about Davis."

"He brought another visitor? Your daughters should be happy to have one each."

"Indeed, my daughters are quite *unhappy*. He brought a *girl!*"

"A . . . girl? You mean a—a *lady friend?*"

"No, nothing romantic. She's a between-age thing named Cathy. An uncultivated sort and such a blatant contrast to my own polished daughters! She is dressed in a most unfashionable manner, and her shoes are as big as sailboats and—"

"We don't criticize people for what they wear, Mabel."

"I don't understand your son at all. He calls her his 'sister.' This chumminess with all strata of society is what he's learning at school! Where he got her, I don't know, but I demand that you insist on him taking her away this very day! And before dinner won't be too soon! We have neither room nor time for charity cases!"

"Well, Mabel, I would have to know more about the circumstances—"

"I've told you all you need to know."

"Our hearts must not become callused by worldly selfishness. After all, this is the Christmas season: a time of giving and sharing with those less fortunate than ourselves."

"Don't preach to me, Ed Dillingham! *I'm* not the transgressor! I've been home burning my face over a hot stove to feed all of you! It's your son who needs the sermon! *You* should have taught him that it's rude to bring people unannounced, and on holidays no less. It'll mean extra work for me and *much* inconvenience to Pearl and Matilda, who should be enjoying the best years of their lives!"

"I'll speak to Edward about it, Mabel. Please calm yourself down."

Ed Dillingham started into the sitting room, then stopped and looked about, confused. He caught at the door frame to keep himself from falling as the world swam out of focus. "Lia!" he mumbled, rubbing his hand across his eyes, for slumped on the couch was a miniature of the woman he once loved. "Lia, you've come back?"

Mabel heard the commotion and saw Ed totter. "You have been drinking, Ed Dillingham!" she accused.

94

"No, Mabel . . . I just . . . I just . . . had a vision or . . . or something. Where's Edward? *Edward!* Oh, Edward, come here! This vision won't go away!"

Mabel shook him roughly. "I will not tolerate a drinking man! Do you hear me? My first husband drank, and you will *not!* I will pitch you out into the street."

"*Edward!*"

Edward came on the run. "Christmas gift, Pa! I brought your daughter home to you for Christmas!"

Mabel shoved her way past Ed. "The joke has gone on long enough, Edward. It's no longer amusing! Wherever you got the girl, you'll take her right back. I insist!"

But Ed didn't hear her; he had eyes only for his long-lost daughter. "Edna! My little Edna!" he cried, stumbling toward her. "Is it really you?"

"It is *not*." Mabel tried to intercept her husband. "Her name is Cathy and she is—"

Ed flung her aside, and her arm hit the wall, bringing a framed picture down with a crash.

"What's happening?" Pearl and Matilda rushed in, looking from Ed to Mabel.

"I've just found her!" yelled Ed, gathering Cathy into trembling arms. "I've been out praying that I'd not have to spend another Christmas without her. And God answered my prayer!"

"Oh, Pa! I love you!" whispered Cathy. "And you look . . . you look even *prettier* than I imagined!"

Matilda—to whom nothing was sacred—stumbled over Pearl in her hurry to get out of the room and yield to her shameless laughter.

CHAPTER THIRTEEN

Davis

Ed was absorbed in his new world of happiness while Mabel seethed with wrath at the unforeseen turn of events. She looked into the future, saw Ed's partiality to Cathy, and made her plans accordingly. There were more ways of plucking a chicken than scalding it first; it could be done one feather at a time. A man's plans couldn't withstand a woman's wiles. She'd bide her time, but she'd have her way. Her own girls would come out as victors. Ed would never talk her into including his children in the inheritance.

Ed added gifts to the volume under the tree for his daughter. He also insisted that Cathy have a proper wardrobe, and with a pleasing facade, Mabel told him that she would handle everything. A country bumpkin like Ed didn't notice details of women's clothing; it took *sophisticated men* to appreciate quality. She'd have the dressmaker "make over" some of Pearl's outgrown dresses for Cathy. There was an old brown delaine that Pearl hated and a cotton muslin Matilda had discarded. *That ought to satisfy the girl,* Mabel told herself, *since it will be better than anything she had when she came.*

Determined that her daughters should have every advantage in the luring of Davis, Mabel felt provoked when Davis noticed Cathy or spoke to her. She watched for every opportunity to turn the channel of attention to her own offspring.

Cathy, feeling the love of her father and blind to the hatred of Mabel and her daughters, walked about in an aura of bliss. She had some pleasant reflections of her own, not the least of which was Davis. Upon learning that she was Edward's sister, Davis's voice and manner were affectionate as he tucked the lap robe about her on the coach and kept asking if she were comfortable. The robe warmed her, but his solicitude warmed her more.

She longed to be able to join in the festivities of Christmas and remembered the three handkerchiefs with the hairpin lace in her coat pocket. They would be just right for her stepmother and stepsisters! If she could get some colorful thread, she would stitch each of their initials on the linen.

Pearl and Matilda gave Cathy little attention, focusing their courtesy on Davis. They sang and played the pianola for him, hovering about with many little favors. Jealousy was not in the weave of Cathy's fabric, and she was glad to see them happy. Marriage was not in her mind, and if it had been, she would have marked Davis off as out of her reach.

Once when Davis lingered to talk with Cathy, Mabel whispered in her ear, "For heaven's sake, Cathy! Don't show your ignorance by claiming anyone's concern for so long!"

Cathy blanched. "I'm sorry," she said. Then unconsciously and half aloud: "What shall I do?"

"Do about what, dear?" asked Davis.

"Cathy is shy, and the notice of a young man makes her uncomfortable," explained Mabel. "But my Pearl is accustomed to entertaining gentlemen, and she'll be glad for an audience with you at any time."

Davis looked into Cathy's troubled eyes just before she dropped them.

Mabel's contriving grew bolder and more obvious as Christmas neared. She asked Davis to drive Pearl to the general store for saleratus to rise her dough. She sent him to help her bring sweet potatoes up from the cellar. She abandoned them together anytime she could while Pearl took advantage of every opportunity to promote herself.

Christmas Eve found Pearl beside Davis on the sofa, dressed in a pale blue satin gown with pearls interwoven in the curls of her raven hair while Cathy's tresses framed her face with glaring plainness. Pearl waited expectantly for a gift from Davis—and hid her disappointment well when she got none. It was harder to conceal her dismay, however, when Cathy got a small bottle of perfume from Davis and thanked him with sweet gratitude.

Cathy's eyes sparkled with girlish delight with each gift she opened, bringing a kindred response from the givers. Edward gave her a pair of Boston slippers, and her father bought her a beaded handbag with a miniature comb and mirror set inside.

But Cathy's unbridled joy was short-lived. She hadn't smelled the garbage fermenting around the corner. After Pearl and Matilda went to bed that night, they talked loudly enough for her to hear, making her aware that the humiliation was intentional.

"They only gave Cathy those gifts because they were

sorry for her," Pearl said. "She plays on people's sympathy with those big, liquid eyes. I could never abide girls like that!"

"I'm returning my handkerchief to her tomorrow. I wouldn't carry a *rag* with those initials!" Matilda said. "M. D. *I'm* not Matilda *Dillingham*. I'm Matilda *Norse*. Dillinghams are nobodies. Norses are somebodies! Our own papa was a distant relative of the King of Norway! Papa-Ed wouldn't have anything if he hadn't married Mama. He was a candidate for the poorhouse when she rescued him! And if Cathy thinks *she'll* get anything that belonged to our papa when hers is dead and gone—"

"Do you suppose, Matilda, that Papa-Ed bought those fancy gifts for Cathy with *Mama's* money?"

"Most certainly he did! That's what I call a wicked and dishonest man! A thief! But from now on, he'll not take what is *ours* and give it to *her.* Mama said she'd see to it."

"And where does Edward get his money?"

Cathy placed the pillow over her head so that she could hear no more. It was too awful, and her stomach was sick. She must talk to her father and ask him never to give her anything at the expense of his "second family." She had not come to upset anything; all she asked was a place to live and a chance to serve others.

However, when she did mention it to her father the next day, he seemed surprised. "Cathy, you are entitled to as much of my income as anyone," he said, taking her hand in his. "You are my flesh and blood, and I'm sure no one could object to my caring for you."

"But . . . but Matilda said . . . it was her mama's money. That is, I mean—"

"I have my own lumber business, Cathy," Ed

explained. "I make a good wage and provide well for my family. I set a bountiful table. Although the house belongs to my wife, the income is mine. I've given no one a reason to complain in all these fifteen years."

Cathy soon found that speaking to her father was the wrong thing to do. Matilda and Pearl got wind of it and cornered her.

"You're trying to make trouble already," they accused.

"I'm trying to *prevent* trouble," argued Cathy.

"If there's anything we won't tolerate, Cathy Dillingham," Pearl said, "It's a tattletale. We say what we wish in the privacy of our room, and nothing is to go outside those walls. *No one* likes a squealer. We've learned that you'll run to Edward or Papa-Ed to be petted every time your little feelings are hurt. If this continues, we'll get even and it won't be pretty. There's two of us and only one of you, and we'll make you out a liar."

"This is *our* house," reminded Matilda. "If you don't like it, we have an uncle who runs a poorhouse. We'll be glad to give you a recommendation to go there."

"And another thing," Pearl added, "While you're making moon eyes at Davis—who is much too old for you— you should be helping poor Mama in the kitchen. Nobody appreciates a lazybones."

After Cathy's ears took in the whole and comprehended that there was no affinity between herself and her stepsisters, she had a wild longing to recall time. To be back in the hut at Roby with Catherine. To erase all knowledge of a brother or a father. The scornful curl of Pearl's lips and the half suppressed ridicule of Matilda were too much to bear!

Suddenly, she turned and fled from the house. With no

thought of destination, she ran until she came to a cemetery, where she fell to the ground and burst into a flood of tears. When she left the poorhouse, she'd fled from a bear and met a lion. Was there no place of peace and goodwill on earth? Were there no guiding stars, no singing angels, no caring shepherds?

For several minutes she sobbed so loudly that she did not hear the sound of approaching footsteps. It was Davis.

"Don't cry so, Cathy." He gently lifted her. "Look up and talk to me. I'm sorry you lost your mother, and I know that you've come here to visit her grave. It's right that you should weep for her. But she is in a beautiful place, and we'll meet her again on Resurrection morning." He took her hand, and she did not withdraw it. "Do you know Jesus, Cathy?"

"Yes. That is, I know *about* Him. Grandmother read to me from the Bible, and I . . . I try to talk to Him every night. It's hard now, but—"

"But it will be better when you have your own room. Do you have a Bible?"

"No, sir."

"The 'sir' isn't necessary unless you wish. You can call me Davis. And I'm going to give you a Bible before I go back to school."

"Oh, no—"

"I have more than one."

Davis had a peculiar way of drawing people out, and as he talked to her softly, he bade Cathy tell him of her early life: the humble house with its low roof, the bare walls and the plank floor covered with rag rugs, and of herself as a bare-footed little girl gathering mesquite beans and cactus pears for jelly. She told of her grand-mother's last moments and of her experiences at the poorhouse. Tears came anew, and Davis, without consid-ering the propriety or impropriety of the act, drew her closer to himself, wiping away the tears, smoothing back the stray curls that had fallen over her face.

As soon as possible, Cathy withdrew from him, saying they should go back to the house. Mabel's caustic reminder that she should not occupy one's attention for long still haunted her.

"But there is one thing that I must know, Cathy. Do you care for me at all?"

"Oh . . . oh, yes! You're the . . . the nicest man I've ever met. That is, besides my father and my brother."

"I know you're young, but I've come to love you. I have two and a half years of schooling yet. You will be near eighteen when I finish. I'd like to take care of you forever—"

"Oh." Cathy didn't know how to respond; she finished with, "That would be nice."

"Will you wait for me, Cathy? Will you be my sweet-heart, and may I write to you?"

"Oh . . . oh, yes . . . Davis!" Her heart thudded with excitement. Davis loved and cared for her!

What Cathy didn't know was that Davis had been fol-lowed—and that Pearl's green and envious eyes were watching them from behind a clump of sumac bushes.

CHAPTER FOURTEEN

Correspondence

Cathy moved into Edward's room when the young men returned to Tarlton University after Christmas.

"I tell you it isn't fair, Ed Dillingham," Mabel carped. "Neither Pearl nor Matilda has ever had a room of her own. I've implored you to let Pearl have Edward's quarters for a full four months now. She's in line for her privacy next. But no! You allowed *your* daughter, Cathy, to horn in ahead of her!"

"Mabel, I did nothing of the sort. It was Edward himself who offered his bedroom to his sister. It is his room, and he can let it out to whomever he chooses. Had he wished Pearl to occupy it, it would have been quite all right with me. Now let's hear no more of the matter!"

"Then the least you can do is put that ugly vase that belonged to her mother in the room with *her* so that I won't have to bear the daily eyesore."

"No, Mabel. I'll keep the vase with me until Cathy has a home of her own. I've told her that it shall be hers when I am gone, and we all understand that, I think."

"Don't worry, no one *wants* the hideous thing, Ed. We'll gladly give it to Cathy, yes, even *implore* her to take it. But you understand that your children are to have nothing of mine?"

"Quite well, Mabel, quite well." Bitterness tinted his voice.

Cathy, eager to prove herself useful and earn her stepmother's approval, moved about the house, sweeping, dusting, looping back the curtains, opening the piano for Pearl (she loved to hear Pearl play) and setting the house in proper order. She had a special knack for arranging things, sometimes moving the sofa a little to the right and the large chair a little to the left until she created an eye-pleasing effect. No thanks was required to keep her diligent; she didn't wish to wear a label of laziness.

Now that she had her own room where she didn't bother her stepsisters, life was easier. She was quite content as she read her Bible and prayed, learning more and more about God's love. Davis had penned a scripture in the front of the Bible for her. It was Psalm 66:20: "Blessed be God, which hath not turned away my prayer, nor his mercy from me."

Her mind often replayed the meeting with Davis in the cemetery, and she wondered when he would write to her. As soon as she got the address, she planned to write right back, thanking him for the verse. She could ask her father for stationery and postage and he'd get them for her. Until now, she had been careful to ask for nothing, but supplies to write to Davis would be her one exception. She hugged the memory of Davis to herself. How could she ever be worthy of such a man who loved God and truth?

Pearl waited for a letter from Davis, too. From her position in the brush, she hadn't been able to hear what

Davis said to Cathy, but her wishful thinking convinced her that what she'd seen was an expression of sympathy not to be confused with personal interest. Cathy was visiting her mother's grave, and Davis was comforting her in her loss.

Davis had admitted to Pearl that there was "someone here" he cared for very much. She had taken the statement and hitched it to the rail of her own ego. Of course he was talking about her.

Pearl hovered over the mailbox every day so that when Cathy's letter did arrive, she took it from the mailman's hand. Nor did she turn it over to the addressee. Although the plan didn't form all at once, step by step she decided to make Cathy's mail her own, reading the letters and answering each of them, signing Cathy's name. Davis hadn't seen Cathy's handwriting; he would never know.

Pearl's duplicity came dangerously close to exposure once when she announced at the dinner table that Davis would not be coming home with Edward for the summer as he had planned. He had a tutoring job in Brownwood.

"And how do you know that, Pearl?" Ed asked the question that plagued Cathy's mind, too.

"Oh, I write to Davis!" she quipped, too quickly, her face reddening. "He is a wonderful pen pal. And, by the way, Cathy—he said to give you a hello. He says he loves you like he would his own sister! He's a big-hearted man!"

"Pearl!" cheered Mabel. "I didn't know that you and Davis were corresponding! Why, you've never shared any of those letters with me. But then, they must be quite personal. And that's wonderful! I'm already planning that you shall attend his graduation."

"That's two years away, Mama."

"And by then you will be engaged! Just you wait and see. I knew when he was here for the holidays that he was crazy about you. I told him that you'd make a perfect wife for him!"

"Mama! You didn't!"

"Well, why not?"

Every word struck a raw spot in Cathy's heart. She had been so sure that Davis meant it when he said he loved her. Had she misunderstood? Did he mean that she should live with him and Pearl so that he might care for her . . . forever?

"Why the brown study, Cathy?" asked Mabel.

"I was just thinking," answered Cathy truthfully.

"She was just *wishing*, Mama." Pearl winked at her mother.

In the spring, Ed worked long hours and Cathy saw little of him. The robins sang, the climbing roses and honeysuckle bloomed, filling the air with heavenly fragrance. Cathy often sat in the porch swing, but Pearl watched for the mail and raced down the road for it each day. She'd return with a letter in her hand and flap it toward Cathy, taunting, "Another letter from my dear Davis!"

Late in the spring, Mabel wrote a letter to her brother, Tom Bates. She informed him that Cathy had found her way to Cranfills Gap, and that she wished he'd have kept her at the poorhouse. "My own daughters are suffering embarrassment because of her," she stated. "Ed shows a decided preference to her over Pearl and Matilda." She added that Pearl would soon be engaged to a fine gentleman "both rich and handsome," but she supposed that she would have to vie with Cathy for Ed's attention for the rest of her life. She complained that although Ed was working long hours, he wasn't making enough money. "He could take a few lessons from you, dear brother," she told Tom, complimenting him on his ability to "make the wax drip."

In the summer, Tom Bates answered her letter with some comments of his own. His son Keeper, he wrote, had never forgotten Cathy, nor had he forgiven her for forsaking him. If she had stayed put, she would be married to Keeper now. It might be that he would take the girl off Mabel's hands yet.

Keeper had started to drink too much, he said . . . and that was Cathy's fault for breaking his heart. He was trying to drown his sorrows. He was sometimes ungovernable, but he would outgrow his irascible moods. Every young man went through stages of revelry. He'd seen wild oats cook up as good as tame ones, he said. Marriage would tone the boy down. If Mabel could help with Keeper, Tom hinted, he'd make it up to her in money.

Mabel, like her unscrupulous brother, would do anything for money. She mentioned the letter to Ed. "I have a wonderful nephew in California that I would like to invite for a visit sometime, Ed," she said, trying to be casual. "I'm sure that he would get along nicely with my daughters and yours." Keeper was not from California, and Mabel was careful not to mention the boy's name or that he knew Cathy. If Ed had an inkling that Keeper had romantic designs on Cathy, he would put his back up before she had a chance to "help" Tom with his churlish son and collect some extra money.

"If you invite him, I want to hear no fretting about the added work, Mabel," he said.

"Oh, Cathy has become a marvelous little housekeeper, Ed. I must say that she is more industrious than both of mine put together! She seems particularly adept at such work. Indeed, her talents lie among the pots and kettles!" She gave a short laugh.

"I think, Mabel, that it does not detract from a lady's worth to be skilled in domestic affairs."

To have her way, Mabel was ready to turn whichever way the wind blew. "Not at all. Not at all, Ed. A girl should certainly learn every necessary qualification to be a good wife."

"And that includes a prudent tongue," Ed said.

Mabel pretended not to hear. "And with Pearl getting married soon, Cathy can move in with Matilda and we'll have a place for Tom's son."

"*Tom's* son? I thought you said this young man was from California."

"A slip of the tongue, Ed." She faked a laugh. "Not *Tom's* son. Now why did I say that? It's *Fred's* son."

"Fred? I don't believe you've mentioned a brother named Fred."

"You are most forgetful, Ed. I told you that I have *six* brothers and they're all wealthy."

Tom was Mabel's only brother, but she figured she could as easily invent five more as one more. "We're all scattered from Dan to Beersheba. And oh, I'm so anxious to have my baby brother's son to visit with us!"

However, time and circumstances prevented Tom Bates from sharing with Keeper the news of Cathy's whereabouts. Keeper committed a crime and spent a year in jail in spite of his father's money and influence.

CHAPTER FIFTEEN

The Harvest

Percival Gomer, being several years older than his spouse—and of whom the woman was not worthy—went on to his well-earned reward. Some said the angels were glad to welcome one of their own kind, for anyone who lived with Ruth Gomer had to be winged and haloed. The mortician said that death brought such a smile to Percival's face that "a thousand undertakers couldn't undo it." He died of *natural causes* the newspaper reported, and everyone hoped that it was so.

Tom Bates, proprietor of the poorhouse, saw his chance to pad his bank account. He promptly married Widow Gomer, moved her and her belongings to his place, and sold her house and land.

Ruth had worked for Tom for five years. He paid her ten dollars for every patron she turned over to the poorhouse. With government funds on every "head," he figured he could recover his money in a short time (if he fed them poorly enough). The baby of an unfortunate young mother was Ruth's first "merchandise." Her name was Bonny.

Ruth had brought many more since, and many of

them were plundered unfairly. She could as easily have kept them out as herded them in, but nothing is so cruel as the lust for money, the root of all evil. And Ruth Gomer was bound by that voracious lust.

When Cathy left the home, Tom demanded his money back from Ruth. The girl didn't stay long enough to turn a profit, he said. He and Ruth almost came to a falling out about it since Ruth had spent the money shortly after it crossed her palm and didn't have it to return. Tom threatened to expose her to Percival, and she panicked. She promised him "two new patrons free" if he'd not press her to pay the money back. Percival *mustn't* learn of her job. He'd quote Scriptures, talk about the Great White Throne Judgment, and sentence her to eternal damnation. (She hated his sermonizing because it gouged her conscience.) Besides, Percival didn't approve of women working outside the home.

With Percival scarcely in the sod, Tom proposed that he and Ruth join their resources together and "become millionaires." Dollar signs glittered in Ruth's eyes, and without forethought she agreed. However, she got her fill of Tom's abuse before the calendar turned a leaf. She hadn't seen a thin dime, and her nerves rebelled against the jolt of her new husband's harsh temperament when for forty years she had known only the docile disposition of Percival.

"I want this marriage annulled." Ruth sat in front of Tom's desk and made her demand.

"That's fine with me, Ruth Bates. It'll be one less mouth I have to feed. But where will you go?" he gibed.

"I'm going back to my home!"

"To your home? You have no home but this."

"What do you mean?"

"I sold your house and put the money in the bank."

"But . . . but I didn't *say* that you could sell my house."

"You signed the papers."

"When did I sign the papers?"

"The day we got married."

"I thought that was the marriage license I was signing!"

"That's what you get for thinking—or for not thinking—Mrs. Bates. My old grandpap taught me never to sign anything without first reading the fine print."

"Then if you sold *my* house, I want *my* money back, Tom."

"You're greener than crabgrass in the spring, Ruth. You gave all your rights to me when the justice of the peace united us."

"How much did you get for my place?"

"Seven hundred dollars."

"Such a price? Well, as your wife and bearing your name, I can withdraw it from the bank."

"Nobody gets money from my account."

"At least *half* of everything you own belongs to me."

He laughed, a satanic laugh. "Guess again. Your name is on nothing."

Ruth pondered her predicament, casting an uneasy glance at the leering, hardened man who stared at her with fiendish amusement. He'd won and he knew it. She felt the foreboding of coming evil, and absorbed in belated second thoughts, she shook her head to clear it. *Her* world was coming to an end.

Tears came to her eyes; she couldn't stop them. Drop

after drop they came, falling onto Tom's desk. But they meant nothing to him, and Ruth was beginning to be terribly afraid of the mercenary man she'd married. Already she was sipping from the bitter cup, the dregs of which she was destined to drain.

All night she lay in a sleepless dread, trying to form a plan. What had Percival said? There was always a way out if one would be still and find it. She stretched out on her back, lay very still, and waited. There! Why hadn't she thought of that? She would sell her valuables; they were stored in a second-story room. They would bring enough to get her away from this dreadful place, and she would start over. Never would she work for Tom Bates again!

When Tom went to town the next day, she commissioned some of the poorhouse residents to help her load her belongings on a horse cart. She escorted the workers to the storage room—and found that nothing of value was left. Percival's black powder gun was gone; the silverware and the china were gone. Even the needlework with which Catherine Willis had supplemented her rent was missing. Ruth was as poor as the poorest creature on Tom's poor farm. Day by day, Keeper had taken her precious items and traded them for whiskey!

A racking headache gripped Ruth and took her to her bed. "Oh, Percival," she wailed, "what have I done to deserve this?" But even as she asked the question, she knew.

The wakeful night caught up with her, and she fell asleep. She slept until a frantic Miss Weems came pounding on her door. "Mrs. Bates! Mrs. Bates! The revenuers are here!"

"Go away," Ruth said.

"I reckon you'd better answer their questions."

"Go away."

"They're coming in, Mrs. Bates."

Guns, uniforms, and stern faces appeared beside Ruth, shipwrecking the aplomb she'd tried desperately to hold.

"What . . . what do you want with me?" she asked, pulling the covers up to her chin.

"We've been watching this place for several weeks, madam. There's a still in the canyon, and it's on your property. Do you know anything about it?"

"A still? Why . . . *no!*"

"Do you recognize this photograph?"

She examined the picture they handed to her. "I believe that's my stepson, Keeper."

"Would he run a still?"

"I . . . I don't know. He's a rascal and he drinks a lot. I don't know that he'd make the stuff, but I wouldn't put it past him!"

They turned to Miss Weems. "Have you noticed any pots missing from the kitchen?"

"I . . . I have, sir."

Back to Ruth. "Where is this son of yours?"

"He ain't mine!"

"Is he here?"

"He's sick today. He was too sick to go to town with his pa. I think he's having a hangover. He's in his room."

When they marched the shackled Keeper past Ruth's room, he shot her a murderous look, worsening her headache. Then Tom came home in a rage and accused her of landing his "innocent boy" in jail. When he screamed, cursed and ranted at her, threatening to "beat her to a pulp," her mind snapped.

Tom put her in the ward with the other poor unfortunates, and she ate the same watery broth as they. As the weeks brought on the summer's miserable heat, her husband made no effort to check on her welfare or provide for her comfort. She was as forgotten as those about her. Tom Bates had gotten what he wanted when he got her property; now it was as if he'd never married her, leaving one to wonder how many he'd thus married and disposed of.

Tom's marriage was so short-lived, in fact, that he didn't mention it when he wrote to his sister, Mabel. Nor did he mention Keeper's prison confinement. As soon as he could get the boy released, he'd send him to Cranfills Gap. A change of scenery might do him good.

Ruth wandered aimlessly about the poorhouse, asking again and again if anybody had seen her Percy.

"Did she lose her purse?" the woman who slept beside her asked.

"She must have," replied Miss Weems. "But that may have been twenty years ago."

"My *Percy*," insisted Ruth. "If you find him, tell him to come and get me out of this place."

Miss Weems noticed that storms especially disturbed Ruth. "It's the last and evil days," she would chant. "The Good Book speaks of the elephants raging. It's a sign of the end. I'm sorry, Catherine. I knew that you didn't want Cathy in the poorhouse, but I wanted that ten dollars. Ruth, are you ready for the world to melt with fervent heat?" She'd stop and chuckle. "Why, *I'm Ruth,* aren't I?"

"Poor Ruth," Miss Weems said, shaking her head. "Harvest time has come for her—and she's reaping those tares."

When Ruth was agitated and restless, little Bonny held her hand and sang to her.

Tom Bates visited the jail every day. It was on one of these visits that he shared the news from his sister, Mabel, with Keeper.

CHAPTER SIXTEEN

A Confusing Summer

It didn't take Cathy long to determine that her father was not happy with Mabel nor could he ever be. He had buried his happiness with Lia and was eager to join her. His heart was in heaven, his body on earth.

Mabel nagged him incessantly about finances until his face became haggard and drawn from the long hours spent trying to provide for her excessive wants. There was always something else to buy: new dishes, more modern furniture, faddish clothes. She had never learned that things don't make one happy, and in her search for what her soul craved, she grasped for more and more of the world's goods. Her sense of priorities had long since been lost in the haystack of materialism.

Only Cathy or Edward could bring a smile to Ed's lips, a light to his weary eyes. Were it not for them, he would have had no reason whatsoever for existence.

Cathy anticipated Edward's homecoming in the summer more for her father's sake than her own. Edward had been with him for all these years, fulfilling a father's hopes, while Cathy had only been in her father's life for a few short months.

119

Another bone of contention in the home was religion. Mabel cared nothing for spiritual concerns and resented the fact that Ed took time from his work to attend church. If she had her way, he would be on the job seven days a week to make another dollar for her spending pleasure. Had it been in her power, she would have *added* a day to the week to suck more income from it.

"If I can't make a living in six days, Mabel," Ed told her flatly, "I couldn't make it in seven, either. No one should steal the Sabbath from the Lord."

Mabel's daughters followed her path in life, but Ed felt it his responsibility to see that his children were reared in "the nurture and admonition of the Lord," so he and Cathy went to church each Lord's Day. It was a special day of closeness and fellowship for them. At these times, Ed talked about how lovely it would be when they were together with Lia again. It seemed almost as if he wished himself already there.

Ed felt the same way about tithing as he did about church attendance. To withhold his ten percent would be to sin against his own soul. Mabel had no idea that Ed tithed, or she would have insisted that the Lord had plenty without Ed's help and that Ed should use every cent he made to care for the things of earth and let God worry about Himself. Her irreverence made Ed shudder.

When Edward sent word that he would arrive on Wednesday of the first week in June, Cathy was elated. She got up earlier than usual, straightened the house, and sat on the front porch to wait for his coach. The slatted swing on which she sat still smelled of newly sawed oak. Ed had made it for Mabel for her fortieth birthday, only to have her deride it as an "old homemade thing." But Cathy loved it, and as she swung she thought that Edward had grabbed a pleasant day for coming home. Young green was everywhere, teaming up with the scent of summer. The fields were a maze of brilliant colors against the backdrop of a small hill. It was heavenly peaceful as she swayed and let the time slip away.

Edward rode out with the mail hack, and as Cathy ran to greet him, Pearl almost collided with her in her hurry to get the mail. "Why, you'd think Pearl's skirts were afire!" laughed Edward as Pearl whirled about and headed back toward the house as fast as she came and empty-handed. "I hope that you aren't in such a hurry, Cathy. It's a beautiful day to be outdoors."

"The only hurry I had was for you to come home," Cathy said. "Everything is better for Pa when you're here. Mabel treats him differently when you are around. Edward, our pa is working himself to death—and nothing he does is good enough for . . . them."

"I know, Cathy. I've lived with that fact for all these years. But I'm home now, and I'll help him while I'm here. But, oh, I was about to forget—and Davis would have my neck! He said to give you a kiss for him." Edward lifted Cathy's hand to his lips. "There! I kept my promise." He fished in the pocket of his jacket. "And here is your letter. He said since I was coming anyhow, I could save him a stamp."

"A letter to *me*—from Davis?"

"Don't put on the surprise act, sister! I know what's going on. Davis talks about you in his sleep! He can hardly wait until the holidays to see you again. A more love-bitten man I've never seen. But then, as I look upon you, I can't blame him."

Cathy said nothing, but her heart lurched. Why had Davis waited so long to write? Perhaps he would explain in the letter. His schooling must be frightfully taxing. It was the first letter she had received from him (so she thought), and she could hardly wait to read what he had written.

When Edward went on to the lumber mill to be with his father, Cathy slipped into her room and locked the door so that she might read her letter undisturbed. She opened the envelope carefully, almost reverently, and saw that he had begun with "My dearest Cathy."

The door rattled, and Pearl called in a whining voice, "Cathy, why have you bolted the door *in the middle of the day?* Let me in." Cathy quickly slid the letter under the bed and went to unclasp the latch.

"Did Edward say anything about our dear Davis?" Pearl asked.

"Yes."

"Oh, what did he say? Pray tell me at once! I can't wait another moment!"

"He . . . he sent greetings to me."

"And not to *me?*"

"I shouldn't know. You'll have to ask Edward. He wouldn't have delivered your message to me nor mine to you."

"I thought I would get a letter from Davis today, but I didn't."

"Perhaps you'll get one tomorrow."

Upon learning no more, Pearl soon tired of idle chatter and left. Cathy closed the door behind her, half afraid that Pearl would return to demand the reason for the secrecy. But she didn't.

Cathy retrieved her letter from beneath the bed, and her heart gobbled up every word from its start to its conclusion.

My dearest Cathy, How I miss you! And how I long for the time that I shall see your beautiful face again! It will be as the face of an angel to me.

It was with much misgiving that I watched Edward leave without me, and I assure you that my heart comes along with him to you. However, the teaching job in Brownwood will earn me the added credits that will make my load lighter for the next two years. I want more time to spend in writing letters to you, my dear.

I should be free to come to Cranfills Gap on Christmas, at which time it will be a whole year since I have beheld my queen. It seems like a whole eternity! Time drags so slowly and the wait ahead seems so interminable that I can hardly bear it, but it will be worth it all when we are together for a lifetime and I am able to provide for you as a lady such as you should be cared for.

I have prayed about my decision to make you my companion, and I know it is right. I have little to offer, but God and I will do our best to see that you have no deprivation. When I think that you were once in a poorhouse—oh, my dear, the thought is too painful for me. Thank God, you shall never suffer so again!

I will write to you often. Affectionately, Davis

"Oh, Davis, you did write! You kept your promise to me!" she whispered as she pressed her lips to the letter. Now where should she hide it so that no prying eyes would find it?

Edward slept under his mosquito netting on the back porch where it was cool, refusing to let Cathy move from his room. He'd be out and gone early anyhow, he said, helping his father with the timber.

A month of the summer passed, and Cathy heard nothing more from Davis. She noticed, though, that Pearl watched both her and the mailbox more closely than usual. She came in with a letter almost every day. There was no reason why Davis couldn't write to both of them, but it did seem strange to Cathy that Davis would write to Pearl so much more often.

With Edward at home, evenings became merrier to Pearl and Matilda. For Ed, the threads of life were only becoming tangled. Mabel's jealousy reared its monstrous head again, and she badgered Ed worse than ever.

"Ed, are you paying your son to work for you?" she asked.

"Edward is earning his own wage, Mabel, with the extra lumber he is cutting and selling. There are plenty of trees for everyone. And they're free."

"But what he earns should be added to the household budget, Ed. We're keeping him, and that counts for something. Just think what we could do with more money."

"My quota of bricks has not diminished, Pharaoh," Ed said dryly. "I'm bringing home no less than before Edward came and started to work with me."

"My name isn't Farrow. Who is Farrow, anyhow? Are you seeing another woman, Ed Dillingham? Are you dividing your living with someone else?"

"Pharaoh was a heartless taskmaster in the Bible. She who hath ears to hear, let her hear. If you think I'm trifling with you, follow my footsteps from before sunup until

124

after sundown and see for yourself. That is, if you can pull yourself out of bed before noon!"

"My point is that Edward should pay room and board if he is making a wage."

"He is sleeping on the porch. And if you insist, he can move to the hayloft. I planted an extra row of everything in the garden this year so that we wouldn't be short of food. The cow gives plenty of fresh milk for us all. What expense has Edward been, Mabel?"

"It's the principle, Ed! You aren't training your son properly when you let him freeload."

"Would you expect Davis to pay for his board? Will you charge your nephew from California rent to stay here when he comes?"

"No, Ed, but I—"

She found herself talking to the wall. Ed had walked out.

CHAPTER SEVENTEEN

Cousin

By winter, the letter that Edward had brought to Cathy from Davis was worn threadbare with reading and rereading. Cathy had ever word memorized and could recite it forward and backward.

As Christmas neared, Pearl became cross and irritable. She snapped at Matilda, cried at the slightest provocation, and pouted in her room. However, when Edward came home alone, saying that Davis had a fever and his doctor forbade him to travel, Pearl's grouch lifted. She seemed relieved that Davis did not come. It made no sense to Cathy.

Edward again brought a kiss from Davis, but since Cathy had received no word from him in the past six months, she received the secondhand affection with mixed emotions. Her cheeks flushed with a feeling she could not define. Edward interpreted her reaction as deep pleasure. Davis had asked Edward to assure Cathy that he would come to see her during his summer break from school.

"Is Davis gravely ill, Edward?" Pearl asked guardedly. "That is, is he in any danger?"

"I think not, Pearl. Just a temporary case of influenza thinks the doctor. He should be well enough to attend classes when they commence again. I had to hog-tie him to keep him from coming along in *spite* of doctor's orders," he broke his sentence to smile at Cathy, "but he'll be here this summer *for sure.*"

Disappointment and confusion met together in the parlor of Cathy's mind. It had been such a long while since she had seen Davis that he seemed little more than a figment of her imagination. Even the picture she had of him in her mind was slowly fading.

When the gifts were distributed on Christmas Eve, though, there was one from Davis to Cathy: a handsome hairbrush with a red rose inlaid in mother of pearl. It was a thing of beauty, something she would prize forever. And didn't a red rose mean love?

She had not thought to get Davis anything, and upon considering it now, she didn't know if it would be a proper thing for a lady to do. Yet when Edward returned to Tarlton with a present from Pearl to Davis, Cathy felt guilty. It should have been she instead of Pearl sending the gift. She was even more frustrated when Edward wrote her a note telling her that Davis liked his gift. By now, she was thoroughly perplexed.

Pearl, realizing that her fraud would be uncovered when Davis came during the summer, confessed the whole deceit to Matilda, imploring her for help and understanding. "I have been getting Cathy's letters and answering them with her signature," she sobbed. "I do want that handsome man so badly, Matilda!"

Matilda was glad to be a lawless confederate of her sister. She had no scruples and, blood being thicker than water, agreed to aid Pearl in cutting Cathy out of Davis's life and slipping Pearl in. "Do not fear, my sister," she said. "You hold the winning cards. It's just a matter of shuffling them to your advantage."

Their answer came in a letter from Tom Bates early in May outlining his intentions of sending his son to Cranfills Gap for "a much needed vacation." The boy, he said, had "worked hard" for a year and deserved a break. After many parleys, he had given his approval for Keeper to do whatever he wished about marrying Cathy.

"That's our answer, Pearl!" crowed Matilda.

"Cathy isn't a bad-looking lassie. Our cousin just might lose his heart to her."

"We can dress her in some of our own pretty clothes."

"I could set her hair."

"Mama will wonder at our sudden friendship when we haven't been exactly chummy with her these two years."

"Mama will know what we're up to."

"She'll help us!"

"But will Mama consider Cathy good enough for Uncle Tom's son?"

"Mama won't care as long as Keeper gets Cathy out of *your* way so you can have Davis."

"You're right. She always said the end justifies the means. And I just *know* Davis will love *me* when Cathy is out of the picture. He'll be so *pleased* when he finds that it is I who have written all those sweet letters to him. Why, all these months, he has asked Cathy in the letters to tell me hello!"

"But what about Papa-Ed?"

"What do you mean?"

"We may have troubles there. He's squeamish about his little Edna-baby."

But Ed Dillingham was not destined to be an obstacle. He met with an accident on his job and went to be with his beloved Lia, throwing Mabel into a spasm of worry over finances. Before Edward could get himself home to take care of things, Mabel sold the lumber business for a price much below its worth, saying that she must have enough money to finish out the year. Then she supposed it would be time to find another widower, hopefully one who had lots of money.

Cathy grieved for her father but rejoiced that his wish had been granted. He had expressed his desire to join the wife of his youth, and Cathy knew that he had found peace and happiness again. She was glad that he was out of Mabel's manipulations.

After Ed's funeral, Pearl and Matilda—and even Mabel—treated Cathy with so much kindness and consideration that she wondered at their transformation. Being true herself, she didn't look for guile in others. She had no way of knowing that they were fattening her for the kill.

Edward wrote that he would drop out of school and come to care for Cathy, but she wrote back that she was being treated in such a gracious manner that he must certainly not think about aborting his education on her account. The change in her stepmother and stepsisters, she told him, was amazing.

During her struggle to accept her father's passing, Cathy received no word from Davis—not even a sympathy note—and she puzzled over it. He, who had lost a father, should be quick to respond to the sorrow of another. Pearl still met the postman and received mail on a regular basis; Cathy supposed the letters were from Davis.

Mabel cleaned out Ed's closet, sending his clothing to the charity barrel. She brought the detested vase to Cathy, glad to have it removed from her room. Then with Ed forgotten and money from the sale of the sawmill at her disposal, Mabel became an amiable woman. She and Matilda blended rollicking voices around the pianola as Pearl played, and Mabel tapped her toes to the music.

The air was already charged with excitement when Matilda came in waving a telegram: "Our cousin is coming! Our cousin is coming!" Some of their thrill spilled over onto Cathy.

"Cathy, dear, you can move in with me," Matilda offered solicitously. "I will love having you in my room. Pearl will share Mama's bedroom, and that way our cousin will have Edward's room until Edward and Davis come in. Then the three of them can room together. Oh, won't we have a grand old time! There'll be parties and courting and dances."

"Edward doesn't dance," reminded Pearl.

"We'll two-step him off to bed and do as we please." Matilda wrinkled her nose.

So unsuspecting was Cathy that she didn't recognize Keeper when he came blustering in. The year he had spent in jail had taken the excess weight from him, and he would have been handsome except for the chilling glint in his dark eyes. Mabel's daughters grabbed him and kissed him on both cheeks, leading him toward Cathy for an introduction.

"Cathy, this is our cousin, Keeper Bates! His father runs a poorhouse way out West—"

Had she seen a ghost, Cathy's face could not have drained of its color faster. Her benumbed mind tried to connect everything but failed to connect anything.

"I know Cathy Willis!" Keeper's black eyes flashed fire. "She and I are good friends. My old man told me that she was here, and that's why I came. I'm looking forward to taking up where we left off at the picnic, dolly—"

"Why, Keeper, how nice!" babbled Mable. "Then you'll enjoy your stay here with us, I'm sure."

He made an exaggerated bow. "Most assuredly, I will, dear auntie."

Panic rose in Cathy like mercury in a thermometer. It filled her stomach and reached for her chest. A flutter that wouldn't go away lodged at the back of her throat; she couldn't swallow.

Keeper rubbed his hands together in a victorious gesture. "Ah, but I'm glad that I came. Cathy, you are much more attractive with a little meat on your bones and dressed in those glad rags. You'll do a husband up proud! And I plan to be that man before I leave here!"

Cathy saw Pearl wink at Matilda. There was a frame-up somewhere.

CHAPTER EIGHTEEN

The Wedding

"Who is Davis?" Keeper propped his elbows on the kitchen table and watched Mabel roll out the biscuits for breakfast the next morning.

"He's Edward's roommate at school."

"And who is Edward?"

"Edward Dillingham. He's Cathy's brother. Why do you ask?"

"I found a letter from Davis to Cathy—and I don't like it!" His face was contorted into an ugly threat. "I asked Cathy to marry me two years ago, and if this creep thinks he can come along and take her away from me—"

Keeper reminded Mabel of her own brother, Tom, when he was a young man. She had seen the same twisted look on his face. "You have no worries, Keeper." She handled her nephew exactly as she had handled Tom in bygone years: with a soft answer. "Davis is in love with Pearl."

"The letter is to Cathy."

"It's a very old letter, written before the young man learned of Cathy's engagement to you. When Cathy explained her position to him, he dropped it. Davis is a reasonable gentleman."

Keeper was not quite satisfied. "Why did Cathy keep his letter?"

"Was it hidden?"

"Yes."

"Aw, she hid it from Pearl . . . and then quite forgot about it."

Part of the taut muscles relaxed in Keeper's set jaws. "I don't want to waste any time in making Cathy my wife, Aunt Mabel," he said. "The old man said if you'd help me arrange this marriage, he'd pay you well. He sent along a hundred dollars—"

"Just how soon do you wish to be wed, Keeper?" Mabel saw her chance for some interim financing.

"She promised to marry me before she left Roby. A two-year engagement is long enough."

"Two years too long. Things would have been much less complicated for me—and for Pearl—had you kept her there."

"If I wait, I might lose her again and, in that case, you would lose your money. I can marry her now, and we can come back for a visit later."

"My sentiments exactly. And I'm sure that she is as anxious as you are—"

"She may offer some resistance; she's skittish. It may take some tricking to get her to the parson or JP, but she'll be glad afterwards."

"To be sure."

"One of my cousins might need to go along. To the preacher, I mean—not on the wedding trip."

"We'll handle it, Keeper. Matilda will be glad to go; Pearl has to stay here and get her letters."

"You don't get your money until I get my wife."

Mabel, with thoughts of money churning in her head, went into Matilda's room where Cathy nursed a sick stomach. "I need to talk with you, Cathy," she said.

Cathy said nothing so Mabel proceeded.

"I believe that you have some thoughts of marriage. Is that correct?"

"Yes. But not for another year. He has to finish—"

"Since your father died, I am your legal guardian. By law, I can give you in marriage to whomever I choose. There's no one I had rather see you marry than my nephew. That way, you'll be my *niece* and I'll always be assured of your nearness. Keeper has asked for your hand in marriage, and I have agreed that he shall have you. He tells me that the two of you have been betrothed since childhood. I'm surprised that you didn't tell us! He has decided he doesn't wish to wait another year. He would like for the ceremony to take place right away."

"May I contact my brother, Edward?"

"Let's see. It would take three days for you to get a letter to him and three days for you to get an answer. Counting out Sunday, that would be a whole week. No, that's too much lost time. Keeper has expressed his wishes to get settled right away. At twenty-two, I'd say that is not unusual for a man. He'll bring you back to visit with us later."

"I would think my brother should be my guardian rather than you. You and I are no kin, really."

"Edward would not object to your marrying so *well*. Keeper is in line for a rather large inheritance, and he is good-looking to a fault. Those gorgeous eyes! What else could a woman want?"

"Character and a good reputation," replied Cathy.

135

"Don't be impudent, Cathy. Keeper *has* character, to be sure. And he comes with the highest of recommendations. And money—ah! He is someone such as I would wish my own daughter to marry!"

"Let her marry him then!"

"Why, he's her cousin!"

"You have misunderstood me. I already have plans to marry *someone else.*"

"Who?"

"Davis."

Pearl had stationed herself outside the door to eavesdrop. Now she burst into the room. "Davis is mine!" She set her arms akimbo. "I've been writing to him for *months* now. I had a letter from him just yesterday, and he says he shall take me as his bride as soon as he graduates. You can forget Davis, Cathy Dillingham, *for he has forgotten you!*"

"I . . . I won't marry Keeper."

"You *will* marry Keeper." Mabel took her by the shoulders and shook her but backed up quickly when Cathy began retching. "You will get well and marry him tomorrow. Matilda will ride in to Meridian with you as a witness, and she can take the stagecoach back. Keeper will return the horse and shay as he brings my money, er . . . that is, at his convenience. You will take your clothes and the vase your father left you—and be gone!"

"And I will keep the hairbrush that Davis gave you last Christmas," Pearl announced. "He said your name was put on it by mistake."

Mabel continued. "The girls and I didn't want you in our home in the first place, Cathy. You tried to supplant Pearl and steal her boyfriend. You are a sneak and a thief!"

The more Mabel talked, the more her runaway tongue spilled out the pent-up venom that had gathered over the years against Ed Dillingham and his children. She had hoped for a more plush life than he had provided—and part of the reason for her shortage was the money for the support his own children required.

That night Cathy saw the moon and stars go down. She laid her head on the sill of the window so that the damp air might cool her burning brow. When morning pushed the sun up the eastern horizon, its first beams streamed across that wooden pillow and caught in her mahogany hair, tangled and matted with her tears.

Matilda, shallow and giddy, gathered her stepsister's belongings, asking if she wanted "the ratty old black coat" that she'd worn when she came. Remembering the spoon in its lining—the spoon she had forgotten to ask her father about—she nodded absently. Her fate was sealed and she no longer hoped for happiness.

Mabel made a great show of kissing her good-bye, all to impress her nephew. Pearl pretended to weep at the parting. Keeper, thirsting wretchedly, held his temper in check with the greatest of effort. He would teach Cathy Willis to drag her feet!

For Matilda, the trip was a frolic. She saved the day for Keeper with her silly prattle: humoring him, diverting his attention, telling funny stories. She preyed on his ego, teasing playfully, and covered Cathy's muteness.

It was twelve miles to the county seat, and by the time they neared the white clapboard church on its outskirts, Keeper's black mood had lightened with the kindred spirit he found in his cousin. "I should be marrying you!" he jested with Matilda. "At least you have a wild and free tongue while this soursop here has none at all." He jerked his thumb toward Cathy.

"I . . . I'm sick. My stomach is upset," Cathy said. "Please may I stop at a privy?"

"Stop at a *what?*"

"An *outhouse*, you dullard!" Matilda shouted, slapping him on the back and howling with laughter. "There! Stop. There's one behind that old church."

Cathy took the vase, wrapped in the black coat, along with her. Keeper and Matilda were flirting so shamelessly that neither of them noticed, nor did they see her when she slipped from the private little building into the back of the church, where she found a hiding place in the over-sized pulpit with its curtained back.

When she didn't return in half an hour, Keeper sent Matilda to look for her. The privy was empty and Cathy nowhere to be seen.

The longer Keeper sat in the May heat, the more his craving for liquor intensified and the madder he became. Now he wished to find Cathy only to punish her, to break her. He jumped from the shay and joined Matilda.

"She must have gone into the church," Matilda offered.

"Then we'll go in and flush her out," Keeper said. "I'll lasso that filly! And she'll wish she'd been more coopera-tive when I'm finished with her."

They barged into the old edifice with no reverence at all; Keeper was swearing loudly. "Yes, I'll teach that little vixen a thing or two. Ah, but it will be glorious to tame her! She'll pay dearly for this little game of hide and seek."

"Why would anyone waste their time sitting in a place

like this listening to a stodgy old man read from a book nobody understands anyway?" asked Matilda.

"Beats *me*," answered Keeper. "I'm not churchy. And if Cathy is, I'll beat *her*."

"She is."

They looked under the benches and behind the giant iron heater. Cathy could hear them getting nearer to her sanctuary. She shook so that her foot bumped against the Sunday school bell, sending it into a high-pitched peal.

"Keeper! W-what was that?"

But Keeper had tripped over the altar and sprawled across the floor in his hurry to get to the back door again. "Ooooooo! Oooooo-ooooo!" He clawed and scrambled to get up while Matilda held her skirts and dashed past him. "Ooo-oooo! Don't leave me in here with these spirits!" He begged. "*Matillllll-da!*"

The horse and shay were gone. Keeper and Matilda walked to the courthouse and were married that afternoon.

Chapter Nineteen

Cathy's Verse

The high-vaulted church was cool and quiet, and Cathy's recent tension brought her to utter prostration. Curled into a fetal position, she slept as one drugged.

She did not awaken until she heard the voices of the good pastor and his wife in earnest conversation; they had come to ready the building for the evening church service. With lamps to light and windows to open they moved about hurriedly.

It took a minute for Cathy to get her bearings, then a stab of panic sliced at her stomach again. *Keeper was back! He was still searching for her. He would find her!*

"The Lord is good, Maybell," the parson said, now close by. "I prayed today that I might be instrumental in helping one of His sheep—or a little lamb."

"It's every service that you help someone, Arnold," she said. "God gives you Scriptures that go to the hearts of the people. It makes them know that He is aware of their needs and that He will never leave nor forsake them."

"We are living in a time of great darkness," said he.

"And this church must be a lighthouse in the storm."

Cathy heard the front door rasp open to admit others. She had waited too late to make her escape without being seen. Now she'd have to remain quietly in her place until the service was over.

When the congregation had gathered, the parson invited them to kneel at the mourner's bench, where they sent up long and fervent prayers. Under cover of their supplication, Cathy was able to change positions, relieving her cramped legs. A time of singing followed, accompanied by someone at the wheezy pump organ. The notes swirled about Cathy, wrapping her in their pulsing harmony.

Then there was a testimony meeting of which Cathy could hear little. Her spirit took wings with the worshipers, and presently she felt no fear. What fate awaited her she did not know, but for now she was safe. Keeper Bates could not resume his search for her until the service ended.

When the parson read his text verse, he was so near that Cathy could have reached out and touched him. She thought that her heart would stop when he began with Davis's verse, *her* verse: "Blessed be God, which hath not turned away my prayer, nor his mercy from me."

Had God spoken directly to her, she could not have been more gratified. Davis may have forgotten her, but God hadn't. An embryo of hope entered her heart, and light flooded the dark places of her mind. Would God—could God—deliver her from Keeper Bates yet? Couldn't God do anything; didn't He know everything? That being true, God knew that she didn't want to spend a lifetime with an evil, soul-scarred man.

Cathy heard only a few words of the sermon. The verse did its own preaching, finding its own path to Cathy's soul. God wasn't a God of mere coincidence, and of all the verses in the Bible—and there must be thousands—the parson didn't choose this one verse by happenstance. This was a divine assurance that God in His mercy would help her.

Her mind raced ahead to the days to come, asking, searching. Deliberating on the complexity she had pulled God into and wondering how He'd get her out, she was unprepared for what came next. At the conclusion of his message, the pastor opened the pulpit's curtain to look for a collection plate—and found her in her hiding place!

He jumped back and gave a startled cry. "Saints, pray!" he beseeched, his face ashen. "Somebody has murdered a girl and stuffed her body in the pulpit! Oh, God have mercy on the killer! And dear Lord, take not your mercy from us, your children, now!"

Women began to moan, hiding their faces and gathering their children about them. Two or three of the men ran to the front, gingerly lifting the curtain to look in on Cathy. "Don't touch the corpse!" warned one. "The sheriff will want everything just as it is for his investigation."

Cathy tried to move, and her heel hit the Sunday school bell again, bringing the terrible jangling. The parson's wife threw up her hands with an outcry: "Oh, Arnold! It's the death knell!"

Abashed to be the cause of so much chaos, Cathy climbed from her covert, stiff from the huddled stance and weak with hunger. "I . . . I'm sorry," she said, not knowing how to begin to make amends. "I . . . I overslept. I should have been out and gone before your service began." A dropped pin could have been heard in the shocked silence. "But I thank you, true man of God, for the verse. It was for me."

With her coat that concealed the vase in her arms, she headed for the back door, surprised to find that night had fallen so completely.

"Well, Arnold!" exclaimed Maybell aloud, "God sent the lamb you asked for . . . and now it is our duty to help her." When he made no reply, she hurried out the door after Cathy.

The half-told story went home on the lips of the small congregation in varying editions. One understood that the girl had been kidnapped and that she had broken away from her captor and hid in the church. Another said no, she was separated from a traveling group in a horse run-away. Still another vowed that she was on her way to her hometown to be wed, but her intended groom got cold feet and dumped her off at the church. No one could explain why she was in the pulpit.

Arnold and Maybell Tucker took Cathy home with them, promising asylum. But the strain had taken its toll on Cathy's overburdened emotions. She collapsed and lay in a stupor, beset by a raging fever, for more than a week.

"Aren't you glad that God can trust us with a lamb, Maybell?" Arnold Tucker asked.

"Yes, Arnold, I am. I used to wonder why God gave us no children of our own. Now I know. It's so that our arms can be empty enough to eagerly receive anyone He sends for us to tend."

"You do think she will be all right, Maybell?"

"To be sure, dear. Else why would God have sent her to us?"

Days and nights passed over Cathy in a blur of drinking from a cup held by gentle hands and the sound of imploring prayers. She swam in a sea of uncertainty, connected to reality by the thinnest thread of consciousness. Mrs. Tucker's face loomed and faded. The real and the imaginary fused inseparably into a dreamless netherworld.

At the end of the week, she was able to smile a small thanks to Maybell and, with the encouragement of the shepherdess, found sure footing for her rationality again. She found the woman a good listener.

"Both my mother and father are with the Lord," Cathy told her. "My stepmother was determined that I should marry a godless and beastly man. God helped me to get away from him, and he's probably searching for me yet."

"He shall not find you!" Maybell Tucker declared stoutly. "As the blood on the doorposts protected the children of Israel from the death angel, I claimed your safety under my roof when you first came. Here, let me read the Scripture that God gave me just this morning concerning you:

"'He that dwelleth in the secret place of the most High shall abide under the shadow of the Almighty. I will say of the LORD, He is my refuge and my fortress: my God; in him will I trust. Surely he shall deliver thee from the snare of the fowler, and from the noisome pestilence. He shall cover thee with his feathers, and under his wings shalt thou trust: his truth shall be thy shield and buckler. Thou shalt not be afraid for the terror by night; nor for the arrow that flieth by day.'

"That's Psalm 91. Now listen to verse eleven: 'For he shall give his angels charge over thee, to keep thee in all thy ways.'"

"I think, Mrs. Tucker," Cathy smiled, "that you must be one of those angels."

"And oh, dear child, listen to the end of the story! 'I will be with him in trouble; I will deliver him, and honour him. With long life will I satisfy him, and shew him my salvation.'" She closed the Bible. "I can hardly wait to see what God has in store for you, Cathy."

Cathy laughed. "All He has for a start is a willing heart, an old black coat, and a vase."

"That's enough. And speaking of the vase, you kept asking for it when you were ill. It must be very special to you."

"It belonged to my mother. She painted it."

"It is beautiful."

"Thank you. My father thought so, and since that's the only thing he had as a memory of her, he wanted me to have it."

"Naturally. Did you know, Cathy, that some pottery becomes more valuable with years?"

"This is a common piece, I'm sure."

"Even so, its value depends on the potter. Most potters put their name—or a stamp of identification—on the bottom. Let's see who made yours." Mrs. Tucker turned the vessel upside down. When she did, a roll of bills dropped onto the floor.

"Why there's money in the vase, Cathy. Did you know that?"

"No, ma'am."

Maybell shook the vase, and more money tumbled out. There were 858 bills stuffed into the vase, a dollar for every week of Cathy's life. Since her birth, Ed Dillingham had stowed them there for her.

The first thing that Cathy did was give her tithe to the poverty-bitten parson. He had never been blessed with such a windfall, and he went out that very day and bought his wife a new hat.

Cathy allowed that it would look good atop Maybell Tucker's halo.

CHAPTER TWENTY

Concerns

When the horse brought the shay home empty on the same day it left, Mabel went into a fit of anxiety. What had happened to the passengers? All of Cathy's belongings were still in the shay: everything, that is, except the outgrown black coat she had insisted on taking and the vase. When three days had passed and still no word had been heard from anyone, Mabel began to weep and wring her hands.

"Oh, pooh, Mama, they'll be back. They're on a lark somewhere!" scoffed Pearl. "They're all old enough to take care of themselves."

"Some tragedy has surely happened to them," bellowed Mabel. "I just feel it here." Her hand went to her throat.

On the fourth day, Edward and Davis came in from college. Pearl and Mabel both tried to talk at once, explaining the reason for Cathy's absence.

"Slow down and start at the beginning," Edward said. "I can't make heads from tails of what you are saying."

"Oh, something dreadful has happened to them!" Mabel said.

"If anything had happened to them, you would have been notified by now. As you were saying, they went into town: your nephew, Matilda, and Cathy?"

"Y-yes."

"What was their purpose for going? Groceries? Cowfeed? Supplies?"

Mabel looked at Pearl and Pearl looked at Mabel, each waiting for the other to explain, to break the news to Edward.

"Well, you see, my lovely nephew came in from . . . from California." Mabel didn't know how much Cathy may have told Edward about Keeper. She deemed it wise to tread softly. "Before he had been here a full week, Cathy fell madly in love with him. They just *matched.*"

Davis gave an involuntary gasp.

"Now before you censure her, Edward, you must know that he was a most personable young man, capable of stealing any woman's heart. He wasn't a trifler, though. He had eyes only for Cathy and she for him."

Beads of sweat formed on Edward's forehead.

"They went to town to be married four days ago. Matilda went along to be Cathy's bridesmaid. Matilda planned to hire a hack to bring her back home after the wedding."

"Cathy . . . married?" Edward looked puzzled.

"Oh, she got a most wonderful man, Edward. Exceedingly handsome and with an adequate income to support her. They were truly crazy about each other. Surely you wouldn't begrudge her—"

"I wouldn't begrudge my sister one day of happiness, Mabel. The Lord knows she deserves it. But I can't understand why she couldn't have waited a week more so that

150

Davis and I might have met her fiancee. She knew that we were coming."

"I suggested that she wait," lied Mabel. "Truthfully, I did. But my nephew needed to get back to California in a rush, and Cathy couldn't abide his leaving without her. I told her that I would make it right with you. You were her only concern."

Davis had said nothing at all, but his face wore a pinched look, his lips spread to a thin line.

"Then I suppose all we have to worry about is what has become of Matilda," Edward said.

"I . . . I suppose so."

"I told Mama not to get in a fret," chirped Pearl, cutting her eyes coyly toward Davis. "We'll hear from her soon. Mama is being modest about Ke—" She caught her mother's frown just in time to withhold Keeper's name, "my cousin's *magnitude*. He's filthy rich! Likely as not, he hired Matilda as Cathy's personal maid at a sum so staggering that Matilda couldn't resist. *I* say the reason the shay came home with Cathy's old clothes is because Ke—" she almost did it again, "our cousin wanted her to have all *new* things. We'll probably get a letter saying that very thing in tomorrow's mail."

That evening, Pearl tried all her feminine charms on Davis. She played the pianola, chattered tiresomely, and trailed her perfume all about him. When Edward mentioned retiring for the night, Pearl asked for "just a few minutes" of Davis's time.

"I know of your affection for Cathy," she said. "We were very close, and she shared some of your letters with me. If there is anything that I may do to make the blow of her marriage easier for you, I shall be glad to try."

151

"When one's dreams meet with sudden death—" Davis shook his head, unable to say more.

"I know, my *dear, dear* Davis. It's hard to believe what a dreadful thing Cathy did to your heart. I have feared this would happen, though. I knew her better than anyone else, and I could have told you that she couldn't be trusted, that she was a fickle little thing. But you would not have believed me."

"You're right. I wouldn't have believed it."

"All the while she was writing to you, she was engaged to someone else. Such two-timing!"

"It is hard for me to accept."

"You never had a hint, Davis? In any of the letters?"

"To be truthful, I did often question the letters. They didn't sound like Cathy at all. The wording didn't sound like something she would write—"

"In what way do you mean?" She made her eyes large and round.

"The letters seemed artificial and pretentious, not at all like the spontaneous and humble Cathy *in person*. When I talked to her—here—I was so *sure* that I was right in my choice, but when I read her letters, I would almost—"

"Almost *what?*"

"Change my mind."

"Were the letters not satisfactory?"

"Oh, I suppose they were pleasing enough—after the carnal mind. But there was a spiritual element missing. Cathy never mentioned God or our fellowship with Him, and that is so important to me."

"I see." Indeed, Pearl began to see where she had failed.

"Maybe I expected too much from Cathy. She was quite young."

152

"Three years can make a big difference in one's maturity level. *I'm* almost three years older than Cathy."

"I . . . I guess I'll never find anyone to take her place."

"You wouldn't have to look far, Davis." She moved closer to him.

Davis bade her to have a good night, and Pearl went to bed heady with success. However, the next morning he took the coach back to Stephenville to his alma mater. The letters to Cranfills Gap ceased.

Edward, on learning that his father's business had been carelessly sold, made preparations to move out. If Cathy had married well, he would have only himself to care for, and that would be a simple matter. Cathy could contact him at school if she wished. He supposed that the separation during their earlier years made her independent and she did not care for his supervision now that their common tie—their father—was no longer around.

It took him some time to sort through and pack his childhood relics, books and paraphernalia from his bedroom and the attic. He had almost finished the job when Keeper and Matilda came home unsteady on their feet, their breath strangely scented.

"This is my nephew, Keeper Bates, Edward." Mabel made the introduction with some trepidation while Edward searched for a memory of the name that was just outside his mind's reach. "He's your new brother-in-law. But where is your bride, Keeper?"

"She's right here, Mabel ole gal!" Keeper pulled Matilda close and gave her a slobbery kiss. "Meet your new niece, Mrs. Dillingham. This is Mrs. Matilda Bates, wife of Keeper Lee Bates, Esquire!"

"Keeper, please be serious!"

"He is serious, Mama!" Matilda insisted. "Serious as consumption. Your nephew is now your son-in-law. Your daughter is now your niece. You're now my aunt-in-law and Pearl is my cousin! Isn't that nifty?"

"Where is Cathy?" Edward demanded.

Keeper shrugged. "We don't know. Do we, Matilda? We took her with us as far as Waco, and she took the shay and left us stranded. Her idea of a shivaree!" Keeper had hardly known a sober moment since Cathy made her escape, and it was doubtful if he actually remembered where he last saw her.

"Keeper, you planned this all along, didn't you?" accused Mabel, with a shaky laugh. "You just used Cathy for a blind—"

"What you don't know won't hurt you, will it, Momsie? But we're raving hungry. This daughter of yours spent all my money and yours the first day. Get in there and fix us a grand wedding feast and let's whoop it up! I brought the drinks!" He looked sideways at Edward. "And sorry, old buddy, that you didn't get me for a brother-in-law. Your loss, I'm sure." He tried to make a bow, got overbalanced, and almost fell over headfirst. "When you find your pious sister, offer her my apologies."

"If you are who I think you are, I shall congratulate her," Edward said coldly. "I now bequeath to you my room, my bantam rooster—and my stepmother." He gave a mocking wave. "And may you all live happily ever after. Good day." Edward gathered his belongings and left, never to return to Mabel's house.

He rejoined Davis, and the two of them searched for Cathy throughout the summer, combing the city of Waco and its suburbs. But they found no trace of her.

CHAPTER TWENTY-ONE

The Job

"I cannot return to my stepmother's house," Cathy told Maybell Tucker. "I dare not take that risk. Anyhow, she let me know that I am not welcome there. I must find a job and earn my own wage. With the legacy Pa left me, I will have a good start."

"Oh, dear lamb! God sent you to us, and you will stay as long as you wish. With the tithe money you've given, we can live grandly for a long time to come."

"I'm grateful for your hospitality, Mrs. Tucker. Indeed, you've been most kind. But I must go to another city. If I stay here, sooner or later I will be discovered."

Cathy had volunteered no information about Edward or Davis, feeling that Mrs. Tucker's lack of knowledge was insurance for her. The thought of Davis and his plans to marry Pearl still brought pain, but the hurt was of her own making: she'd read too much into Davis's single letter, his brotherly words at the cemetery.

Edward would insist on caring for her if he knew her circumstances, but Cathy could not bring herself to interrupt his education. With the swift changes of modern times, higher learning was a necessity. Edward had only two years of study left, and it would be unfair of her to disturb them.

Deep inside, Cathy felt as alone as she did the day her grandmother left her. So much had happened since then that she seemed separated from Catherine's simple life by a thousand ages of time. All the happenings since creation might have been wedged between her and the woman she thought was her mother. Even the memory of Catherine paled like a time-faded photo. Centered between sixteen and seventeen, Cathy felt like a very old woman, carrying the weight of the world on her shoulders, rolling a great stone endlessly uphill.

"We'll pray about a job for you, Cathy," Maybell promised. "God knows where to place you. I only hope that it isn't *too* far away! I cannot bear the thought of not being able to see you now and then."

The opportunity for a job opened that very week, giving Cathy the impression that Mrs. Tucker's prayers had their own telegraph line straight to heaven. Maybell's twin sister, Fay (christened Faybell, but she'd dropped the "bell"), came from Fort Worth for her annual visit. In conversation with Maybell, Fay learned of Cathy's need for employment.

"I know where there is a job opening," Fay said. "It was listed in the classifieds, and my neighbor called it to my attention. The pay is excellent: fifty cents a day plus room and board. But I'm afraid it isn't an enviable position."

"I will take anything so long as it is honest work," spoke up Cathy.

"Oh, it's as honest as soapsuds and dustpans can be!" Fay laughed. "It's a maid's job for one of the wealthiest old coots in Tarrant County. They say he hires a different servant for everything: to keep his grounds, to drive his carriage, to cook his meals. Gossip has it that he even hires one servant just to wash his windows—and that there are more than a hundred windows in all.

"But he's miserably hard to work for! Claims are that he's possessed of foul moods, sudden mind changes, and harsh demands—and he's eccentric besides. He's never been married, they say. Lives in a mansion in Benbrook. He runs through servants like a schoolboy runs through shoes: wears them out and needs new ones every few weeks! Then he puts an ad in the newspaper—"

"It couldn't be any worse than working for Miss Weems," Cathy said.

"Who is Miss Weems?"

"The taskmaster at the poorhouse."

"The poorhouse? You worked at a *poorhouse*?"

"No, I lived there; there were no wages."

"Oh, my precious lamb! Those places are instigatated by the devil from the pit!"

"And staffed by his imps," put in Fay.

"The government contributes to graft and corruption when they support such a program—"

"Don't get Maybell started on that!" laughed Fay. "That's her hobbyhorse."

"No *child* should ever be in a poorhouse."

"I am very much interested in the job for the poor old fellow," said Cathy.

"Rich old fellow," corrected Fay.

"Money doesn't make one rich nor does poverty make one poor," pointed out Maybell. "Man's life consisteth not in the abundance of the things he possesseth."

"And that's another favorite subject of hers," Fay said to Cathy. "I declare, my sister should have been a preacher herself; she can 'most nigh out-sermon Arnold!"

"I really must go and see about the job right away." Cathy tried to draw the conversation back to the original topic. "I can get along with almost anybody, and I've had plenty of experience with soapsuds and mops."

"Well, if you'd like, you can ride back to Fort Worth with me," Fay offered. "Benbrook is very near to Fort Worth. In fact, I'll be glad to take you over for an interview."

"How far is it from here?"

"About sixty miles as the crow flies, about seventy as the road bends."

"That's far enough away, isn't it, Mrs. Tucker?"

"In a city so large, you'll never be found, Cathy. And I'll feel much better if my sister accompanies you." Maybell sighed. "I know you're old enough to care for yourself, but you *seem* so young to a thirty-six-year-old woman. And anything that's small enough to fit in a pulpit—!"

"In a *pulpit*?" Fay pulled her brows together. Then the pulpit story had to be related to her. It so amused her that she declared it "fit for a nickel novel."

Cathy was anxious to move on. With the fear of exposure, she left the Tuckers' home only for church services. She rested poorly and had recurrent dreams of being captured and tortured by Keeper Bates. It was an immense relief when she took her leave with Fay at the end of the two-week visit.

On Monday morning, Cathy stood at the imposing front door of Colonel Evans, as the townspeople called the affluent bachelor. His residence usurped a whole city block, standing at some distance from the street, from which its massive walls, wreathed in evergreen, were just discernible.

An iron fence surrounded the whole, and the wide, cobbled walk passed through a heavy gate guarded by huge bronze lions so natural and lifelike that Cathy distanced herself from them. Leafy oaks grew in proliferation with a lush lawn spread beneath.

The house itself was of stone—two stories and surrounded with a piazza whose pillars were entwined with morning glories, honeysuckle, and rambling vines. At the left was a well-kept flower garden, blooming with an endless variety of shrubs. A goldfish pond, over which a small footbridge had been built, reposed in the midst of the garden.

Just the kind of place one reads about in books, Cathy thought, pondering the irony of the extremes in her life: from the poorhouse to a mansion. For standing here now looking over the premises, she knew in her heart that she would get the job.

While Fay waited by the curb to see if Cathy would be hired, a tailored butler ushered Cathy into the interior of the drawing room to see Mr. Evans who, she was informed, never hired anyone without speaking to them in person. For a few moments, Cathy stood transfixed. The magnificence about her was even greater than her concept of heaven.

Mr. Evans entered promptly. He stood tall but was a sparse man with thinning hair who walked—did everything—with fast, jerky movements. He sized Cathy up for a brief time without speaking; she met his eye with a confident air. Hadn't God sent her here?

159

"So you think you want a job here, young lady?" His tone was caustic but not altogether inhumane.

"Yes, sir, I'm *sure* that I do."

"You don't look strong enough to carry a dinner tray."

"I'm stronger than I look, sir."

"And older too, I should hope."

"*I* think that I look exactly my age, sir."

Mr. Evans' moustache twitched. "And what previous experience have you had, Miss—?"

"Cathy Willis. I mean, Cathy Dillingham. That is, my legal name is Edna Dillingham, but my grandmother, who I thought was my mother, called me Cathy and I'm not used to being called Edna, so—"

"So you haven't answered my question. What experience have you as a maid and what wage are you accustomed to?"

"I have no *formal* training, sir, if that's what you mean. I haven't taken any classes in dusting and mopping. I worked in the kitchen at the poorhouse for a short while."

"At the *poorhouse?*" Mr. Evans exploded. He banged his fist on the table. "You should *never* confess that to a prospective employer."

"I'm ashamed of nothing that is honest work, sir."

"And what were your wages at the, er, at *that* place."

"None, sir."

"None? Are you telling me that you worked for *free*?"

"After a manner, sir. Yes, sir."

"That's too many sirs in one sentence. What other recommendations come along with you?"

"Grandmother taught me to embroider, but she's dead. I kept my stepmother's house spotless, but Pearl and Matilda didn't like me, so their report might not be accurate. And I helped the parson's wife, Mrs. Maybell Tucker."

"At what wage?"

"I've never earned a wage, sir." She looked at him with a girlish grin. "And please notice that that was just *one* sir, sir."

Mr. Evans made a great effort to keep his face straight. "Can you give me a bit of history? I like to know the background of the people who work for me."

"I've no pedigree, sir. I'm a country girl from a simple background, and there isn't much to tell."

"You have nothing to offer?"

With childlike openness, Cathy told Mr. Evans about her grandmother, Catherine Willis, and then about her trip to Cranfills Gap to meet her father, Ed Dillingham. After his death, she didn't want to be a burden to Mabel Dillingham, who had two daughters of her own. She had one brother, Edward, in college in Stephenville, but she didn't wish to bother his education with her own care, she said.

Mr. Evans seemed too distracted to listen. He drummed his fingers on the cherry wood table waiting for her to finish her monologue. His fidgety motions were greatly accelerated by the time she had finished.

Cathy sensed that she'd lost his attention and stopped abruptly. "Is that enough?" she asked.

"Quite sufficient. I said *some* history, not a genealogical exegesis on your whole clan! Actually, I am interested in knowing if there are any criminals in your family: thieves or murderers or outlaws that would be visiting you?"

"Not that I know of, sir. We all seem pretty honest to me. Edward said Pa once made him take a marble back to a boy at school. I . . . I hope that he wasn't gambling. . . . Anyway, I'm not expecting any visitors while I work here."

Mr. Evans sniffed. Cathy couldn't tell if it was a suppressed laugh or a sneeze. "Gaither!" he shouted, and a short militant man with a ledger appeared as if by magic. "Give this lassie a list of maid duties, make ready her living quarters upstairs south, and make a note that she will be bringing my meal trays to me."

"And the wages, sir?"

"Put her down for seventy-five cents a day. And pay her once a week."

"How much did you say, sir?" His eyebrows shot up into his shock of unruly hair.

"You heard me correctly."

"But none of the other maids—"

"Gaither!" thundered Mr. Evans. "I conduct my business to my own liking, and no one has the right to question me! Another word and you will be replaced!"

"Pardon, sir." The man looked frightened, but Cathy felt no qualms.

Mr. Evans turned back to Cathy. "Will that wage be sufficient?"

"Oh, it's *much* too much, sir."

"Too many muches in one sentence." The old man almost smiled.

"If it will cause problems, please lower it!"

"You will have more duties than the other maids."

"I will work very diligently, sir."

"And if you will give me an address, I'll send a cart for your belongings."

162

Now Cathy laughed aloud. "I have an old black coat, a vase that belonged to my mother—and God."

Mr. Evans seemed suddenly uncomfortable; he turned his head away and was silent. "That should be enough," he said at last. "I furnish uniforms for my maids. The seamstress will measure you this afternoon."

Here his mood changed. "Have a good day, Miss Edna Willis, Cathy Dillingham, Edna Dillingham, Cathy Willis or whoever you are." He was poking fun at her, but she didn't mind. She had the job—and at such a wage!

Cathy returned to Fay. "I got it!" She rejoiced, reaching into the buggy for the coat and the vase that held her money. "And Mr. Evans and I are going to get along *royally!*"

CHAPTER TWENTY-TWO

Bonny

Earning such a wage, Cathy thought she would be content. She had never been so well cared for nor so comfortable. But something ate holes in her peace of mind: something she couldn't quite place.

She thought at first that it might be Davis, but upon searching her heart, she found no jealousy for Pearl. She laid all the blame for her heartbreak at her own feet, a foolish girl assuming too much from a friendship.

Her unrest didn't seem to concern her brother, Edward, either; she felt she had made the proper decision there. The problem that scratched at the door of her mind went back farther than Davis or Edward.

Then she had the dream. Or was it a vision? In the dream, little Bonny came to her with upraised arms, pleading with Cathy to come and take her away from the poorhouse. There were tears in the child's eyes, and then she became smaller and smaller until she was no more. Cathy awoke and prayed for Bonny, but when she went back to sleep, the dream was repeated exactly as before.

A conviction—more like a premonition—settled over Cathy that Bonny would not long survive in the poorhouse. Children needed proper nourishment not only for the body but for the spirit as well. But what could a teenage girl do for a six-year-old child?

The feeling that all was not well for Bonny grew to such proportions in Cathy's mind that she could hardly concentrate on her work. She remembered a particular verse of scripture in the New Testament that now grated on the nerves of her soul: *But whoso hath this world's good, and seeth his brother have need, and shutteth up his bowels of compassion from him, how dwelleth the love of God in him?*

If that verse was for her, then she must act on it. How could she obtain Bonny's release from Tom Bates? The man would not give her up willingly. She was four dollars a month in his pocket. The child meant nothing to Tom, but the money did. However, Tom liked lump sums; he couldn't resist ready cash. That was something for Cathy to work on. She had the money that her father left to her . . .

Mr. Evans had been gone for several days. Bookkeeper Gaither said he had been "out on business" and that before he left he was particularly crotchety. "If the old man isn't making money, he isn't happy," said Mr. Gaither. "Frankly, I'm glad when he's gone."

"Mr. Evans needs to learn eternal values," Cathy suggested. "I'm praying that he will find life's greatest treasure."

"Save your prayers, miss," Gaither said. " 'Twould be easier for a camel to be stretched into thread for a needle."

When Cathy made her decision about Bonny and knew that she was doing what God was calling for her to do—she asked for an audience with Mr. Evans. Without a spiritual perception, he would not understand. *He's my boss, but he isn't my Master, she told herself. God is my Master, and what He says to do, I must.*

"I've come to give my resignation, Mr. Evans," Cathy told him. "I will be leaving tomorrow."

Mr. Evans was peeved. "Are you not pleased in my employ?"

Cathy didn't waver. "Oh, very, sir! But I have a higher calling."

"Where are you going?" His voice was gruff, his eyes hard.

"I'm going back to the poorhouse—"

"I will not allow it!"

"—to get a little girl that will surely die if I don't rescue her. I've had two dreams, and I know that God is talking to me—"

"Is this child related to you? *Yours,* perhaps?"

"She is in no way related to me, sir. Except to my *heart*, that is. We shared the same quilt while I was there."

"How old is she?"

"She's about six years old, but she's no bigger than four. Her name is Bonny—"

Mr. Evans pounded the table with his fist, a habit of his. "I've never had any children, and a fretting child would drive me to pure madness!" he yelled.

"Oh, but you have misunderstood me, sir! I am not asking that you allow me to bring little Bonny *here*. I wouldn't think of imposing on you! I am *resigning my position* with you today and will be leaving in the morning."

"How will you support this child?"

"I . . . I will find another job . . . and . . . well, I don't know just yet, Mr. Evans, but God will lead the way. He will open a door. I am doing this for Him."

"I can't let you leave without proper notice. And one day isn't enough."

He was trying to hold her, and Cathy knew it. The reasons were beyond her comprehension since he could replace her with two more for the awesome wage he paid her. But she did not back down. "This is a free country. I came to you of my own accord, and I shall leave in the same manner, sir."

She arose to leave.

"Sit down!" he barked, and she obeyed. "Will you return to this area?"

"I really don't know, sir. That depends on several factors, but I should hope so."

"I have checked your references. You do have a brother at Tarlton College. Your stepmother lives at Cranfills Gap. As to your grandmother, I was not able to find out anything about her, but I have determined that you are a girl of your word." He paused. "Before I give you your wages for this week, I want you to make me a promise."

"I don't make promises before I know what they are, sir."

"Bring the little girl by to see me when you get back."

"If I come back and if you wish, I will do that."

"Who knows, the child might even *like* me." The old man's words were acid laden, and Cathy pitied him. "Ha! No one else ever has!"

"Why, I like you, sir. You have been *too* kind to me. But even if I had no care for you, *God* does."

Mr. Evans gave no indication that he had even heard her. He turned his back and didn't speak another word.

Cathy took her money from the vase and tucked it into her clothing. When she was ready to leave the next morning, she was surprised to find Mr. Evans's coachman prepared to take her to the depot.

"Mr. Evans says that you are to go by train rather than by coach," the man said. "It is much faster and more comfortable. He has provided a round trip ticket for yourself and a return ticket for a child. The berth and meals are included."

"But . . . why?"

"He is a man of many strange quirks, miss. None of us ever try to outguess him or his maniacal actions."

By the time the heaving iron monster growled its way onto the West Texas cap rock, spitting fire and smoke, Cathy had made plans and counter plans. She was prepared to meet Tom Bates. She was sure Keeper wouldn't be there; he was still searching for her in the cedar breaks around Meridian.

When she presented herself at the poorhouse, Tom greeted her cordially. He asked the welfare of his sister, Mabel, and his son, Keeper. "I no longer live at Cranfills Gap," she told him. "I have been gone from there for some time now. I know nothing of them or their welfare."

"Then you have come to await Keeper's return?"

"No, Mr. Bates. I have come for a child who lives here. Her name is Bonny. I plan to take her away with me."

She met the resistance she expected. "I don't turn my residents out to the mercies of the world, Miss Willis. The government pays me to keep them here, and that is what I shall do."

"Yes, Mr. Bates, the government pays you four dollars a month for each person. You have at least forty, and that nets you 160 dollars a month. Bonny is almost six years old. If she stays until she is twenty-one, you may expect to collect 720 dollars on her. However, if she doesn't live, you've lost 720 dollars. Without proper nourishment, children tend to die young. If Bonny should marry outside the poorhouse or run away before she reaches adulthood, you have lost forty-eight dollars a year."

"What is your point?"

"I have come to offer you seven hundred dollars cash for the release of Bonny to me today. I will make the offer once and once only." She arose to go.

"Wait! Where are you going?"

"I'm going to see Bonny before I leave."

Tom Bates followed Cathy to the ward, keeping her in sight as if she might evaporate in midair along with the promised money. Cathy found Bonny weak with a fever. Tom looked at the child warily; she was no more than a pack of bones. "For the sake of her health, I think that you are right, Miss Willis. You should take the child with you today. Please come to my office, and we'll fix up the papers." He started out ahead of Cathy.

On the way out of the ward, Cathy passed an empty-eyed woman rocking back and forth on her pallet. "Hey!" she hailed Cathy. "Have you seen my Percy?"

Cathy hesitated. The woman bore a striking resemblance to Ruth Gomer!

Miss Weems noticed Cathy's shock. "The woman is as batty as a bessie bug!" she said. "The planting of bad seeds brought her here like the planting of good seeds took you away from here."

Tom looked back, greatly irritated. "Are you coming, Miss Willis? I haven't all day."

Cathy left Roby with her till almost empty but with her heart full. She had rescued Bonny just in time; the child couldn't have lasted much longer. However, with good food and a lot of love, Bonny would soon regain her health. How she would provide for herself and this helpless child, she did not know, but God had a plan. He would lead her. . . .

A nameless peace settled over Cathy as two small arms slipped around her neck. "I said my prayers every night and asked God to send you, my Cathy. I thought that you'd *never* come."

Now, God, besides the black coat and the vase, here are two more items for you to use as raw material for a miracle, prayed Cathy in her heart: *a frail child and a tattered quilt.*

Winter was coming on.

CHAPTER TWENTY-THREE

Head of the Household

W hen Cathy and Bonny arrived at the Fort Worth station, Bonny's fever had dropped, and she had taken enough nourishment to strengthen her. A coach waited to take them back to the Evans mansion.

"The day you left, the colonel told me to watch for you every day and see you home safely," the coachman told Cathy.

"Mr. Evans is a kind man."

"Many would dispute that, I'm afraid."

"I will miss working for him."

"None of us will be working for him much longer."

"What do you mean, sir? Is there a boycott?"

"No, he had a stroke shortly after you left and has been near death's door since."

The news greatly disturbed Cathy. If she knew that Mr. Evans had made preparations for eternity, she told herself, she could be glad for him. But her father said that what one was *after here* determined one's *hereafter.*

The doctor met Cathy as she went to her room to gather her belongings for departure. "Is your name Cathy?"

"Yes, sir."

"Mr. Evans keeps calling your name. Please stop by to see him before you leave; it might do him good. In any event, it won't do any harm. He's not long for this earth."

When Cathy and Bonny went into the sickroom, Mr. Evans showed no signs of consciousness. "Talk to him," the doctor said. "Some of my profession claim that comatose patients can hear."

Cathy moved to the bedside. "Thank you, Mr. Evans, for the train tickets," she said softly. "I got little Bonny—"

Here the child took Mr. Evans's limp hand. "Poor, poor sick man," she said with a child's simplicity.

"Look, Cathy, he has a tear!" she said. From the corner of Mr. Evans's eye came a crystal droplet.

Bonny bent over and gently kissed the leathery face. "God can make you well, our dear Mr. Evans!" His eyelids made a tiny flutter but nothing more.

"We mustn't tire him, Bonny," Cathy said. "He is very ill. Come along. We need to find us a place before dark." She went to her room for her coat and vase, and the coachman offered to take her wherever she wished to go.

"Could we just drive about until we find a small boardinghouse in a common part of town?" Cathy asked. "I can only pay a small rent. I will be obliged to you for your time and trouble."

"At your service, miss." He gave the horses a flick with the reins and took her to a modest neighborhood not far removed from the mansion.

"Oh, this area will be much too expensive for me!" she said. "Are there no more economical areas?"

"There are the slums."

"Take me there."

"I'd worry about you there, miss. There are mice and vice."

"God will take care of us."

As they turned down a narrow side street, she saw an unpainted house with a placard in the window: "Rooms for Rent Reasonable." Underneath was scrawled "Vacancy." Cathy knew she'd found their lodging. "Just set us out here, please," she said, offering the driver a coin for his trouble. He waved away the tip and left mumbling that "them youngsters need earthly caretaking to go along with the heavenly."

Up two flights of rickety stairs, in an attic room that overlooked an alley, they made their home. Cathy spread the frayed quilt and the black coat on the cot, and Bonny immediately availed herself of the bed and fell asleep.

Cathy, her mind spinning from the events of the last few hours, stood studying Bonny's tiny white face, so white that the blue of her closed eyes showed through the lids. Blue veins streaked her temples and her hair tumbled into a thousand golden ringlets. She was a beautiful child! A lump came to Cathy's throat. "Thank You, God, for helping me to rescue her in time," she breathed. "It was worth giving up all my savings."

The magnitude of her responsibility hit Cathy. What if Bonny should become severely ill and need medical attention? What about her education? Her clothing and shoes? How could a girl who had not yet reached her seventeenth birthday have the wisdom to guide a six-year-old to adulthood?

"I'll need to get her a doll or a coloring book," Cathy told herself. "She'll need something to occupy her time while I am at work. Oh, how I'll hate to leave her! But, of course, I must. I can't do much for her, but the little that I can do will beat death in the poorhouse."

The child stirred and awoke, a cherubic smile spreading over her face when she saw Cathy watching her. "Well, this is our home, Bonny," Cathy cheered, and the child clapped her hands joyfully. "But you understand that I will have to work, don't you?"

"You won't leave me, will you?"

"Only for a few hours each day, but I'll always come back."

"Why must you work?"

"So that we can have bread and milk, a place to live, and heat for the winter. All that takes money."

"If I am a bother to you, Cathy, then I can go back—"

"Oh, no, sweet thing! You are no *bother.* I would have to work anyhow even if I were by myself—and it will be so much more fun to have someone to come home to! But you'll have to be nice and quiet while you are all alone."

"I will be nice and quiet. I cross-my-heart promise, Cathy. But I won't be *all alone.* God will be here with me. And Cathy?"

"Yes?"

"Every day I'll pray for dear, sick Mr. Evans. And God will make him well."

Cathy picked up day-old newspapers from the manager of the apartments. She watched daily, fearing there would be a notice of Mr. Evans's death. A man of such wealth would command a large obituary in the *Fort Worth Star Telegram.* Day after day, she found no mention of Mr. Evans.

By stretching what little money she had left from her father's gift and taking any jobs she could find, Cathy managed to get them through the winter. For several weeks she was employed at a sewing factory, which proved a great blessing. She was able to bring home enough scraps to piece together string quilts for the cold weather, and looking ahead to Christmas, she saved back the larger pieces of material to make gifts.

It wasn't a lavish celebration, but Cathy managed to make the holidays special for Bonny. She cut up one of her own muslin petticoats to make a doll for the child, using the black coat's buttons for eyes. Out of small squares of cloth, she made a patchwork dress for Bonny's baby and a bonnet to cover her hairless head. They had no tree, but Bonny helped Cathy twist red and green strings together to hang in the window for decorations. Together they made hot-water taffy, and on Christmas Day, Cathy told Bonny the story of the baby Jesus born in Bethlehem and laid in a manger.

As the cold weather grew weaker, Bonny grew stronger, a healthy pink coloring her cheeks. Cathy, careful not to neglect her spiritual obligations to the child, took her to a nearby church every Sunday. Bonny thrilled to every spiritual aspect of the worship, but the music was her greatest delight. She drank deeply from its fountain, swaying dreamily to its cadence.

In the spring, Cathy gave one brief thought to Davis's graduation, supposing that he would soon be wed to Pearl. Edward now had one more year of school, after which she planned to make contact with him. Even he may have chosen a wife by then.

All in all, she had much to be thankful for, but she knew that her pitiful wage would not sustain them much longer. Her reserve was going fast, both financially and physically. It was time to have a heart-to-heart talk with the Master.

Chapter Twenty-Four

The Two Calls

For several months, Edward Dillingham had felt his call to preach. Thus when he met up with Parson Tucker at a church convention and the good pastor invited him to come to Meridian for their summer brush arbor meeting, Edward knew it was time for him to launch his ministry.

The return to a town so near his boyhood home would be taxing since he'd lost both his father and his sister nearby. After more than a year, he had found no trace of Cathy, and now he feared that there had been foul play in her disappearance. If she were alive, she would surely have contacted him before now. Edward didn't know Keeper Bates, but during the short acquaintance he sensed the depths of evil in the young man's spirit. He was a slave to alcohol.

Both Edward and Davis had prayed for long hours that they might be led to Cathy, but they seemed to find no answers. Davis was inconsolable, and Edward knew that the grief of his roommate was no less than his own. Finally, they had committed the problem to God, and each in his own heart more or less gave her up as forever gone from their lives.

The weather was perfect for a June revival. Willing hands went to work dragging up shrubbery for the shelter, setting posts, accumulating piles of leafy branches for the arbor's top, and hanging lanterns by their wire handles. They constructed a crude platform and scattered sawdust underfoot to keep the dirt from flying. The wooden benches from the church were hauled across to the lot with the mourner's bench taking the center front position. When the pump organ was moved in and the pulpit set in place, it looked churchy.

People came from miles around, and for the duration of the meeting, several families camped by the creek that ran nearby. The revival was going well, and some of Edward's nervousness due to being a novice had fallen away, when a strange thing happened.

Brother Tucker reached into the Bible stand for a song book, and a rat jumped out. The parson almost flew over the pulpit in his fright. Several in the congregation arose from their seats with a start. Edward thought for a moment that there would be a mass exodus of these distracted folks.

The remainder of the service was wrecked by what Edward considered a minor incident. Minds were scattered, and he was unable to pull the audience back into a unity of worship. He felt that his sermon was a failure and went to the pastor's house feeling low and defeated. If a mouse leaping from the podium demanded more attention than his message, he must be a poor speaker indeed! Edward was not given to depression, but this affected him.

Mrs. Tucker, a perceptive lady by virtue of her position, sensed Edward's despondency and thought she knew the reason. "Brother Edward," she said, proffering consolation, "you did a mighty fine job this evening."

"No, I . . . I failed," said he.

"Please don't feel that the poor attention of the people had anything to do with you or the delivery of your good message—"

"I could not but think otherwise, I'm afraid."

"It was the rat scare that diverted everybody's minds."

"I didn't realize that congregations were so easily put to disorder or so difficult to recapture," he said. "I have much to learn."

"You will likely never face a situation so irregular, my good man. The people here cannot rid themselves of a terrifying occurrence, and the rat brought it to their memory. About a year ago, at the conclusion of a church service, Arnold raised the curtain on the back of the pulpit to fetch out the collection plate. When he did, he jumped back with a cry of alarm, for inside the Bible stand was the body of a girl!"

Edward drew in his breath with a sharp intake. "A . . . a girl?"

"Arnold thought the lass murdered and hidden there, but she proved to be very much alive. She was in hiding from someone who was pursuing her. She didn't mention names and I didn't ask. What one doesn't know, one doesn't have to recount, you know."

"You . . . you don't know her name?"

"Only Cathy."

"*Cathy?*"

"Do you know a Cathy?"

"Yes! She is my sister. She has been missing for more than a year."

"She didn't mention having a brother."

"Or a friend named Davis?"

"No."

"About how old was this Cathy?"

"In her middle teens I'd guess. As I say, I didn't ask questions."

"Where was she from?"

"I didn't press for that information, either; she only mentioned a stepmother to whom she could not return."

Edward dropped his head into his hands. "Cathy! Cathy!" he wept, releasing his pent up emotions. He raised his face, stained with tears. "And then she . . . left?"

"Yes. My sister helped her to find employment with a wealthy man in Benbrook. I suppose that she is there yet."

"The greatest proof of my commitment to God is to stay here until the arbor meeting shouts itself out," Edward admitted. "Were it not for this revival, I would be on my way to find my sister in the next half hour."

Arnold Tucker offered to release him from his obligation, but in prayer, Edward could not obtain his release from God. And stay he did, for Edward was a man of great self-discipline and fortitude. A sweeping revival broke out, and eighty souls were filled with the Spirit and baptized in the creek at Jackson's Crossing. The meeting ate up most of the summer, but Edward, deeming the spiritual more important than the carnal, spent many hours praying in the grove. He never once questioned his God.

When the meeting ended, he went directly to Fort Worth, learning the address of Cathy's employer from Maybell Tucker's sister, Fay.

The doctor was just coming out of the mansion as

Edward approached, and Edward stopped him. "Sir, can you tell me if there is a girl by the name of Cathy Dillingham who works here?"

"I don't believe there is, sonny." The doctor scratched his head. "There was a lady by the name of Cathy somebody who came for a visit last fall. She had a small child, perhaps four years old—?"

"The girl of whom I speak has no child."

"I'm sorry that I can't be of help to you. Employees come and go here like Solomon's chariots to Tarshish."

"The man who hires . . . he'd know, wouldn't he?"

"Yes, he'd know. But he has had a stroke and hasn't spoken a word for several months. He is such a baffling case, that old fellow! I am certain that he is aware of everything about him and that his mind is unaffected. He can move his arms and legs; I know that he isn't paralyzed. Yet he refuses to try to walk or talk. I'm sure that he *could* if he would just put forth the effort. He's one of those medical mysteries. Something is dammed up inside of him that he refuses to break over.

"The old gentleman is pitiful. He has enough money to buy the city of Fort Worth but no friends. He hasn't had a single visitor since the lady and her little daughter came to see him before the holidays. He has never been married and has no living relatives—which all goes to show you that there's no comfort in riches. Sometimes I think he refuses to get well because he wants *my* attention. Really, he has no reason to live."

"How stands his soul?" asked Edward, momentarily forgetting his disappointment at not finding Cathy.

"Never darkened a church door or breathed a prayer in his life as far as anybody knows."

"Then I shall speak to him about it." Edward voiced his decision aloud.

"I won't be responsible for his reaction," warned the doctor. "But I'll grant that any reaction—even anger— would beat none at all."

Edward, emboldened by a nudge of God's Spirit, went to Mr. Evans's room. The man raised his eyes; there was cognizance in them.

"Mr. Evans," Edward said, without preamble, "I'm Edward Dillingham. I came here looking for my sister, Cathy, but I have a yet greater mission. I want to talk to you about your soul. I don't know you; I know nothing about your past, but God does. And He sent me here. These are the verses of Scripture that He gave to me for you." Edward pulled his Bible from his pocket and began to read from Isaiah: "I have blotted out, as a thick cloud, thy transgressions, and as a cloud, thy sins: return to me; for I have redeemed thee."

"And here is the other. It is in Zechariah: 'But it shall be one day which shall be known to the LORD, not day, nor night: but it shall come to pass, that *at evening time it shall be light.*' "

Mr. Evans said nothing, but tears came to his eyes.

"Do you understand what God is telling you, Mr. Evans?"

There was an almost imperceptible nod of the old man's head. But it was there, and Edward saw it.

Chapter Twenty-Five

Progress

Two things happened that week. Cathy lost her job that paid their rent and Bonny turned seven. Their resources were dwindling, and Cathy was at the point of panic. They would presently be put out on the street.

"I have nothing to give you for your birthday, little friend," Cathy apologized to Bonny, "and not enough flour left for a birthday cake."

"I don't want a *something*," Bonny said. "I just want my bestest wish to come true."

"And what is your best wish?"

"I want to go see dear Mr. Evans and find him with his eyes open. I haven't missed a day making a prayer for him to God, and I dreamed that he can open his eyes now."

"Then we shall go," said Cathy. "Just to please you. But it's a very long way and we must walk."

"I have two ready legs."

At the Evans mansion, the housekeeper escorted them to the old man's room. The doctor had propped Mr. Evans in a chair with several pillows. Bonny made a dive for him and clasped his inert hand in her own tiny ones. "Oh, our dear Mr. Evans, your eyes *are* open!" she cried. "I just knew that they would be! I had a dream that you were all well again—and oh! how I hoped and prayed that my dream might come true!" The man watched the child with alert eyes while the doctor watched his patient.

"Mr. Evans!" the doctor laughed. "This makes two days in a row that you have had visitors. Yesterday the nice preacher man came, and today this lovely lady and her little daughter have come. You are getting quite popular!" The man's eyes moved to Cathy, and in them she read something indescribable. Was it hurt? Mourning? Distress? It almost seemed like a *pleading*. She felt a wrenching around her heart. He was trying to tell her something, and she could not understand the look. If only he could talk!

"I've been wanting to visit you for ever so long, Mr. Evans," Bonny chattered on. "I wish I could see you *every day*, but it's a very long walk to here. I wish you could get out of that chair and take me to see your garden. Cathy told me that you have the most wonderful goldfish! Can you hear the birds singing, Mr. Evans?" She put her small palm up and toward the window. "Did you know that birds sang even before *people?* Listen! I think that's a hermit thrush. Cathy taught me about different kinds of birds and the sounds they make. Her Grandmother Catherine taught her. Oh, it's pretty music, isn't it, sir?"

Mr. Evans moved his mouth as if he wanted to speak, but no words came. "Come on, Mr. Evans, you can talk!" Bonny urged. "You almost did!" The man tried again, making a garbled sound.

The doctor clapped his hands. "That's good, Mr. Evans! See, those vocal cords still work! That's progress!" He turned to Cathy. "Amazing! The child has done in ten minutes what I have not been able to accomplish in six months. I have an idea. I would like to hire your little daughter to work for me for a few days if she may. I'll pay her well. Would it be possible for you to stay in residence with her here and commute to your work? Say, for a month or so?"

"Oh, please, Cathy," implored Bonny. "I've never had a real job, and if he's talking about me watching over dear Mr. Evans, it would be a really, really *fun* job! May I, please?"

Is this why I lost my job, Lord? So that Bonny might help with Mr. Evans's therapy? Cathy asked the questions in her heart and got a resounding yes for an answer.

"I am between jobs just now, doctor. If you need Bonny, we will be glad to do what we can. Both of us are quite fond of Mr. Evans, you see. We'll have to go for our things." She saw Mr. Evans's head tilt ever so slightly, his eyes brightening with an inner light.

"Mr. Evans's driver will take you," the doctor said, and Cathy thought Mr. Evans's head doddered in agreement.

Settled in the spacious south bedroom again, Cathy felt as if she'd come home. Bonny's delight knew no bounds; it was her first experience to sleep on a feather bed. She came up sputtering: "Cathy, I thought I was sinking all the way to China." She wiggled her toes in the carpet. "Oooo! This is heavenish, isn't it, Cathy?" she gushed. "I think it's more wonderful than a *queen's* room!"

The doctor's only orders were that Bonny should entertain Mr. Evans every day and urge him to communicate. Bonny filled her role well.

187

"I'll be glad when you can come out and play with me and Cathy," she told the old gentleman. "Cathy made me a dolly out of her—well, out of some *white material*—and I named my dolly Eva because that's the closest to *your name* that I could get for a *girl* doll. You're just about the nicest man I've ever met, Mr. Evans. Mr. Bates at the poorhouse was *rich*, but he didn't love God and *I know that you do*. I'm glad Cathy came for me, but it was *you* who bought my train ticket." She prattled on merrily, hour after hour.

"Don't you like watching God push the sun up to your high window so you can see it every morning, Mr. Evans? Isn't God wonderful? He sends the moonlight and the stars to wink at you at night, too, doesn't He? I like *up* rooms 'cause they're closer to heaven."

Mr. Evan's hand fluttered.

"Oh, Mr. Evans! You moved your hand. You did! You can do it!"

Each day brought more improvement, and the doctor said that his patient's appetite had "perked up" considerably. He now had great hopes that Mr. Evans would have a complete recovery. He paid Bonny a dollar a day for her "work."

Bonny liked her earnings. "Cathy, I'll soon be as rich as Abraham, and then I can get Mrs. Ruth out of the poorhouse like you got me out," Bonny said. "She begged to be taken out every day."

"Mrs. Ruth?"

"Yes. She lived in town, but when her husband died, she married Mr. Bates. He didn't want her anymore so he put her in our ward and she cried."

"Ruth Gomer?"

"That'n."

Sowing and reaping. That's what Miss Weems meant.

Bonny asked endless questions. Cathy never knew what information the child's active mind would demand next, and it rather frightened her. She wasn't sure that she was capable of satiating the child's thirst for knowledge. With her intelligence, Bonny needed a tutor.

Since Bonny had no roots of her own, she liked to hear stories of Cathy's own childhood and especially about her grandmother who could paint and produce marvelous creations with a needle. Cathy suspected that Bonny relayed everything—good *or* bad—to Mr. Evans. In this, she was correct.

"Cathy's grandmother, Catherine Willis, could paint pictures," she told Mr. Evans one day. "And so could Cathy's own mother. Did you see the vase that Cathy's mother painted? It is *beautiful!* Would you like to see it?"

"Y-yes."

"You said a word, Mr. Evans! You really did! But I'm not a bit surprised. Oh, just wait until the doctor hears about it! Won't he flip his stethoscope?"

The man seemed pleased with himself, setting his lips in a faint smile.

Bonny went for Cathy's vase. "These flowers are lady slippers and moccasin flowers," she explained. "There's rosemary and ladies' tresses, too."

Mr. Evans tried to reach out and touch the vase, and Bonny moved it closer to him, forgetting that reaching was not a normal thing for him to do. To the child, it seemed natural.

"Pret-ty," he said.

"Cathy's grandma could paint anything she saw. I think that Cathy could paint, too, if she had the brushes. Cathy can even make things look pretty with *words*. In the poorhouse, she told me stories and made me forget how cold it was."

The next day, Bonny stood on tiptoe to look out the window. Suddenly she motioned to the old man, "Oh, Mr. Evans! *Come quick!* I wish Grandmother Catherine could have painted *this*—"

Mr. Evans heaved himself from his chair and almost fell to the floor when his unused muscles wavered under him. But he pulled himself to the sill and looked out. A spotted fawn stood under a tree looking up at Bonny. "Isn't he a handsome bambi, Mr. Evans?"

"He is—" Mr. Evans said.

They were standing side by side watching the graceful creature when the doctor entered the room. "Mr. Evans!" he shouted, causing Mr. Evans to whirl about and almost fall headlong. "You are standing!"

"I am, doctor."

When Bonny saw that both Mr. Evans and the doctor were weeping, she began to cry, too.

CHAPTER TWENTY-SIX

Mr. Evans's Story

Bonny's work is about over, Lord. Now what shall we do next? Cathy knelt beside her bed for another talk with the Master. Before the day was over, her answer came.

Mr. Evans asked for a private conference with Cathy while one of the maids took Bonny for a stroll in the garden. His speech had returned to normal, and his limbs, inactive for so long, were regaining their usefulness.

"I owe you a lot, Cathy," he began.

"Oh, sir! You owe me nothing. I think we can attribute most of what has happened to a little girl's determination and prayers."

"But you . . . you started me on the road back to God."

"That is the highest compliment you could pay me, sir."

"May I tell you my story, Cathy? Perhaps the telling of it will drain some of the poison from the cup."

"I am a good listener, sir."

"When I was a very young man, God spoke to my heart and I became one with Him for a short while. Those are the only happy days I can remember. Then God asked me to carry his gospel, but by then I had taken a wife—"

"You were *married*, Mr. Evans?"

"For less than a year. I felt that, as an itinerant preacher, I couldn't provide for my wife as I should. I was torn between two: God and mammon. I'm regretful to say that mammon won. But all peace left my soul, and I began to drink heavily to drown the call of God. One night after a rather silly argument, I demanded that my wife leave and never return. She did.

"I realized my mistake right away, but I was too proud to ask her to come back. And then I heard that she had died in the smallpox epidemic that wiped out most of her family. I became bitter, fighting guilt, and in my recrimination I railed against God for taking *her* when it should have been *me*. I had done the wrong, not she. I shut myself away from God and man.

"I fled to the farthest place I could think of, which was California. I was running from myself, running from God and fleeing memories. I happened to be at Sutter's Mill in 1849 when gold was discovered, and I was one of the few who came away with enough of the accursed stuff to buy Seward's Folly.

"When you have money, Cathy, many people hate and envy you. I delighted in returning evil for evil; I reciprocated with hatred. I was convinced that every employee who worked for me only wanted their wage. No one cared for *me;* it was only my money they craved.

"And then you came. You were different. You even asked that I *lower* your wage. You had what I had lost so many years ago—a oneness with Christ. I could feel it, sense it. When you mentioned God, it made me uncomfortable. It opened up the longing that I thought I had successfully buried—"

"I came because I knew God sent me."

"That He did. And when you left to go for the child, I was afraid that I would lose you. It was with a selfish motive that I provided those tickets. I demanded that my driver haunt the train station until you returned. I never meant for you to move out. Because I had never had a child, I didn't know how I would adjust to one—or, I should say, I didn't know how the child would adjust to a wretched old man like me so devoid of human kindness. Now I don't know how I would have . . . made it without her.

"It seemed that everything about me turned to stone the day you left. I had nothing to live for. When you went away, you took . . . God with you. The emptiness was unbearable.

"When you returned, I wanted to ask you to stay, but none of my reflexes would work, and I was unable to speak. I couldn't even open my eyes so I . . . wept. I had concluded that God no longer cared about me. I had spurned him too long. I had let him down. Why should he bother with me?

"Then just before you came for the last visit, a young preacher came with Scripture from God directly to me. God let me know that He had forgiven me and that I could return to Him because He had redeemed me—and that there would be *light in the evening time* of my life! I still couldn't speak, but my heart did a lot of talking to God after Edward left."

"Edward?"

"Yes, that was the boy's name. And the strange thing is, he had your same surname: Dillingham. Edward Dillingham."

"Mr. Evans! That must have been my brother."

"Yes! The one who was in Stephenville. Of course. You favor. Come to think of it, he said he came looking for his *sister.* I should have put it together then—"

"I'll write to him today!"

"Tell him that the old man got reacquainted with his Savior. And welcome him here anytime."

"I may be gone when he comes, but I'll leave directions where he may find me."

"Where are you going, Cathy?"

"You are doing well. Bonny's services are no longer needed. We'll move on—"

"I have never dismissed you from my employ, Miss Dillingham! Your wages for all these months are in my bookkeeper's office. You may resume your duties any time that your care for the child will allow. We'll hire a nanny for her if you'd like."

"But Mr. Evans, I *couldn't*—"

"But Miss Dillingham, you *could!*" He smiled a smile so whole and beautiful that Cathy thought her heart might burst. "We don't want too many *couldn'ts* in one sentence, you know! Anyhow, your being here will not put me out in the least. The *interest* that my money draws from the bank is enough to run this entire household from now to eternity."

"But Bonny is *my* responsibility."

"Yes, and in that case, *we* need to think about her education. How old is she?"

"Seven."

"She needs a private teacher at least an hour a day. I'll contact the superintendent of schools for the county and ask him to send out the best teacher he has."

"It is *too much,* Mr. Evans. Were we your children or grandchildren, that would be different, but since we are no kin—"

"And there's something else I wish to do. Bonny tells me that you yearn to paint. We'll have an art instructor out here for you, too, while Bonny is studying. She tells me that your mother and grandmother painted, and she showed me a sample of your mother's work on a vase. I was quite impressed. I dare say that painting runs in your family!"

CHAPTER TWENTY-SEVEN

The Quilt

Fall came with its browns and grays, especially for Edward Dillingham. He wasn't at the university when his letter from Cathy arrived; he'd had all his mail held for the duration of his absence. He had gone to Comanche County to work in the peanut harvest in order to finance the remainder of his education.

Heavy rains and high water kept him away from school longer than he anticipated. It seemed that he met with reversals at every turn, and he even toyed with the idea of discontinuing his studies. But he was so near to completion—only one short year to go! Too, it had been his father's request that he finish.

At Benbrook, Mr. Evans converted a parlor on the first floor of the mansion to a classroom for Bonny. Cathy took her painting lessons on the second floor in a room adjoining his own so that he could watch her as she worked at the easel, mixing paint and brushing strokes on the canvas. Who enjoyed their classes better—Cathy or Bonny—would be hard to tell.

Cathy's professor was a busy little man with a heavy accent. "Ah! Meez Cathee, for de professeon you ver *created!*" he preened. "See de nice lines, de deepth per-cepteon? Ah! I make you *famous!* Then you no haf to marry. You be reech vithout de hosband at all!" He slapped his knee and laughed at his own cleverness.

Bonny liked her teacher, too. "I asked him if he believed in Jesus," she told Cathy. "Because I don't want anybody teaching me that doesn't believe in God or that He made the world."

"What did he say?"

"He said that's the reason he was hired—because Mr. Evans asked the superintendent straight out for a *Christian* teacher! He is a very *pretty* man such as I would like for you to marry, Cathy."

It was the second time in one day that marriage had been mentioned, and Cathy felt a twinge of resentment. "I have no plans to marry, Bonny."

"But someday you will become somebody's wife. Somebody would be *cheated* without you. Someone is running around out there just *half* without you. And I've been wondering what *I* should do when you marry."

Cathy had taken note of Bonny's growing pensiveness, and it had caused her some misgivings. So this was the child's worry. . . .

"But Bonny, I told you that I am not getting married."

"Some little voice tells me that you will."

"You'll always live with me, dear child."

"No, Cathy, I think that wouldn't be *right*. You're not old enough to be my *mother*. You seem more like my big sister. You shouldn't start off your marriage with an *already* child. You should have your own."

"I can have my own and you, too, when that time comes."

"But I'd like to live with a *real* family—maybe a parson and his wife—so I'd be next door to God and have a whole stack of Bibles. My fingers just itch to play the pianola or the big organ while someone sings to God! Oh, Cathy, I know I could do it! And wouldn't that be a blessing to some parson to have a daughter who could make sweet music to go along with his wondrous sermons?"

And I know just the parson who would love to have you. . . . Thoughts were coming too fast—and unbidden—and Cathy tried to push them away. She fought the dreadful prospect of parting with Bonny, pummeling the idea with mental fists. But was she being fair to the child to cling to her? She was too young and Mr. Evans too old to fill the little girl's emotional needs. Bonny was right. She needed a *family.* Just because Cathy had rescued her from a wasting death in the poorhouse gave her no claims on the child's future. Oh, how Arnold and Maybell Tucker would love her!

"I know a lovely parson and his wife who have always wanted children but have none—"

"Would we *fit*, Cathy? That's most important. Would they want *me*?" There was real yearning in the child's voice.

"You'd fit like a pair of cozy mittens, Bonny. They'd be so very good to you that you might end up spoiled rotten, and I'd smell you all the way to here."

"No, I'd spoil *them* rotten by being the behavingest child in the world! I'd sit right on the front bench at church and sing the loudest! Oh, when may I go to my parson parents, Cathy?"

"I'll talk to Mr. Evans about it. He'd have to supply the transportation. I'm sure he will want you to finish out the school year before you go."

199

"Teacher is leaving at the holidays anyhow. And I don't want to have to *tame* another teacher! He might not be a Christian. When I get to my new family, I'll be going to regular school with other girls and boys anyhow, won't I?"

Cathy considered it best to present her problem to the Lord first, then to Mr. Evans. She knew the Lord would understand: this might even be in His long-range plan. Mr. Evans would be another matter!

However, when Cathy approached Mr. Evans, he was reasonable. "I don't know how we can do without that little cherub," he said, "but the child's arguments are sound. I'm too old to romp and play in the garden come spring. I may not even be here! And you need to devote more time to your own heart's call."

"It isn't *me* that I'm thinking of."

"If this is God's plan, who are we to stand in His way, Cathy? I've learned my lesson. I went my own way for more than half a century—and look what a mess I've made! If the people who adopt Bonny need assistance, I will gladly support her."

"They are poor, but they will not accept charity, Mr. Evans." Should she say it? Yes. "You could tithe, though."

"I could do what? Tie?"

"Tithe. That's a Bible principle for caring for those in God's work. It is the ten percent of one's increase that *belongs* to God. I realize that in your case it would amount to quite a sum, but one robs God when one doesn't obey His plan. My grandmother, Catherine, set a good example for me. If she painted a picture and sold it for fifty cents, she gave five cents to the church for the parson's keep. She said the other forty-five cents went a lot farther when she did it that way."

Mr. Evans's eyes were upon her, but some third eye went beyond her. Was he upset? "I will do that, Cathy," he said. "From now on until I draw my last breath, I will tithe."

His mind seemed to go on a long journey and then come back. "There's one thing that I want."

"What is that, Mr. Evans?"

"I want the ragged quilt that Bonny brought in to cover my feet one day when I couldn't walk or talk."

"She brought it from the poorhouse."

"She won't need the old thing in her new home! I'll send her plenty of new ones to take its place. I'd like to keep that old quilt as a reminder of the dark days and what God has done for me."

CHAPTER TWENTY-EIGHT

Teacher

Cathy sent Maybell Tucker a telegram saying she'd found them a girl child that she knew they would adore, and would they like to have her? A letter, stained with happy smears of tears, came back the next week. It contained such an outpouring of love and desire that Cathy wept for joy in spite of the ache in her heart.

Bonny spun about in spirals of ecstasy. "Oh, what are they like, Cathy? My ma and pa? Tell me *like lightning!* My ears are *buckets* to hear all about them. Does my new ma have soft mother-hands?"

"Oh, yes, Bonny. That's one of the things I remember the most about Mrs. Tucker. When I was so very ill, those hands held my head as I drank broth."

"And is her voice mothery, too?"

"Ever so much!"

Bonny would be finishing her studies with her teacher in time to arrive at her new home for Christmas. Cathy had heard nothing from Edward, and she dreaded the prospect of her own Christmas without Bonny or Edward. She'd put on a front for Mr. Evans, though. He declared he hadn't celebrated a holiday in a "whole generation of time," and he'd like to try it this year.

"Holidays are for families," he said, "and I have none. But now that you're here, Cathy, we'll have Christmas together."

Bonny sensed Cathy's anguish at the parting. "Don't be sad, Cathy," she coaxed. "You'll always be my sister, and when I've grown up, I'll come to see you every Monday."

Cathy laughed. "Why Monday?"

"So that I can tell you what songs I played on Sunday," she said as if Cathy should have known. Then she changed the subject, an art at which she was adept. "And I think that I'll hate leaving Teacher about as worse as I hate leaving you and Mr. Evans. He is so holiness, and oh, Cathy, I did so want you to meet him before he went away. I had him in mind for your husband!"

"Why, you little matchmaker!" scolded Cathy. "I'm certain that it wouldn't have worked, for there was once someone that I loved dearly, and he married someone else."

"You never told me."

"It's something I don't like to talk about."

Mr. Evans ordered his most luxurious carriage to transport Bonny, escorted by Cathy, to the Tuckers in Meridian. He was not quite strong enough to go himself, he said. Bonny fluttered about, hugging Mr. Evans, then all the household servants, and back to Mr. Evans again. Cathy ran to her room for her handbag, taking the circular stairs two at a time. "Hurry, Cathy! My new ma will be watching for me! I don't want her to be worried on the first day!"

When Cathy returned, her body froze at the bottom step of the staircase, refusing to budge. Her mind jelled along with her legs. For there in the parlor stood Davis with his arms around Bonny!

"Teacher came to tell me good-bye," Bonny bubbled. "Wasn't that a *delicious* thing for him to do?"

In one swift glance, Cathy saw the revolution on Davis's face: from surprise to disbelief to relief, followed by a combination of joy and longing. It was plain, like the reading of an open book.

"Cathy!"

"Do you know my . . . Cathy?"

"Yes, I . . . I do. I met her three years ago, and I wrote her many, many letters when I was in school. My dear Cathy, it is such a pleasure—" He moved toward her, but she backed hurriedly up the stairs in alarm.

"You mustn't be scared of Teacher, Cathy," shamed Bonny. "He wouldn't hurt anybody!"

Oh, how I loved him! But now he belongs to someone else! He is married to Pearl. How shall I ever rid myself of this feeling?

"My little student kept telling me about 'Cathy,' but I had no idea—" It looked as though Davis might come up the steps in pursuit of her, and Cathy looked about wildly for a means of escape.

Bonny ran to her and took her hand. "I told you, Cathy, how *pretty* Teacher was, and how as I'd like you to marry someone like him! Now that you've seen him after all these years, don't you agree?"

Cathy's face blazed with humiliation. Her voice was but a whisper in Bonny's ear. "Shhhh. He's already married, Bonny. He married my stepsister."

"Teacher!" Bonny called out before Cathy could hush her. "You didn't tell me that you were married! That wasn't fair! Here I had you all picked out in my mind for Cathy!"

Now Davis looked confused. "I'm not married!"

What has he done with poor Pearl? Cathy wondered.

"Cathy said," Bonny began, and Cathy put her finger to her lips, which did nothing to stop the child. She barged right on, "that you married her stepsister."

"Her stepsister? Of whom are you speaking, Cathy?"

"P-Pearl." Her lips quivered and she blinked back hot tears.

"Pearl?"

"But you wrote to her and . . . and she said that when you graduated, that—"

"Wait, Cathy. Something is terribly wrong. I have never written Pearl a single letter in my life! I said nothing to encourage her attention or lead her to believe that I was interested in her. *All* my letters were to you." Some dawning broke over the skyline of Davis's mind. "And you answered those letters, didn't you, Cathy?"

"No. I . . . I didn't get but one, and that was the letter Edward brought to me."

"Cathy, I wrote to you every day. Please believe me. Did you never go to the mailbox?"

"Pearl wouldn't let me. She got there first—" A faint illumination started to reach her, too.

"Yes, obviously Pearl helped herself to your letters and answered them with your signature. That's why I couldn't make the letters sound like you. There was never a mention of God or His Word. Oh, my darling, what you must have suffered! How you must have questioned—" He started toward Cathy as she started toward him, and Bonny was caught in the middle.

"Let me out of this *crush!*" the child implored.

CHAPTER TWENTY-NINE

Light in the Evening Time

Davis insisted on accompanying Cathy and Bonny to Meridian. He couldn't get enough of Cathy's nearness and employed various and sundry exploits to keep Bonny from between himself and his sweetheart. He finally *paid* Bonny to sit with the driver in his box.

The day was brilliant with sunshine, but the air was brisk. A becoated Maybell was sitting on her porch when they arrived. She had been there all morning waiting for the "bundle of love" God had chosen to brighten her home.

She had Bonny's room decorated with frilly curtains, her bed piled with handmade stuffed animals. The bonding was so complete between Maybell and Bonny—and so instant—that Cathy suffered no regrets at leaving her. Already Bonny was running her fingers over the yellowed ivory keys of the antique organ in the living room. She had found her earthly haven.

On the way back to Benbrook, Cathy pointed out the old church where she had hidden in the pulpit. "I can see the humor of it now," she chuckled, "but then it was a matter of life or death!"

"Oh, my darling!" Davis exclaimed. "The thought of your pain almost stops my heart! The scoundrel that put you there told us you were in Waco, and Edward and I combed the countryside for weeks looking for you. We gave you up for dead. Why did you not contact us to tell us you were safe?"

"I knew that Edward would feel it his moral obligation as a brother to care for me even at the expense of his education. I thought that I should earn my own wage until he finished his schooling. Then I planned to contact him. But when I learned from Mr. Evans in the fall that Edward was searching for me, I wrote to him at the university. However, I have heard nothing—"

"We'll find him, Cathy. Because he must be here for the wedding without fail!"

"The wedding? What wedding?" She pretended great surprise, but her eyes twinkled.

"Cathy, darling! I've endured three hundred letters from a charlatan! I've worn the knees of my trousers out in prayer for you! Now that I've found you, you *will* marry me, won't you?"

"Is this a proposal?"

Davis pulled out his pocket watch and looked at it. "Right here in Mr. Evans's fancy carriage between Meridian and Benbrook, at three o'clock in the afternoon, this is a marriage proposal."

"Right here in Mr. Evans's fancy carriage between Meridian and Benbrook, at three o'clock in the afternoon, this is my answer." She wound her arms around his neck and kissed him full on the lips. "I'm all yours, Davis—that includes my old black coat, my empty vase, and myself!"

"But brace up, my lady! It's going to be hard to tell old

Mr. Evans that you're leaving. He has grown quite fond of you. But that's not surprising; I'm sure he couldn't help himself." He squeezed her hand.

"Thanks be to God, I'm leaving him in better shape than I found him," Cathy said. "When I came, he was a bitter and disliked old man. He has made peace with himself and with God, and now even his servants love him!"

At the Evans mansion, another surprise awaited Cathy. Edward was there, waiting for her. He had gotten her letter and headed for Benbrook that same day. Tears mingled with thanksgiving at the joyous reunion. There was so much catching up to do, but they'd have the rest of their lives to do it.

Heart to heart, as well as hand in hand, Davis and Cathy went to tell the old gentleman of their plans to wed.

"Will it be soon, Cathy?" the old man asked. "It will be hard to lose you and Bonny so close together. It's like losing . . . my family."

"We won't forget you, Mr. Evans. But soon isn't soon enough to suit Davis and me," Cathy told him. "Edward is here, and we see no reason to postpone our wedding. I'm eighteen now, you know."

"Then we'll have a grand dinner in the dining room tonight," said Mr. Evans, calling for his cook to issue his orders for the meal. "The four of us will enjoy a meal together in honor of your engagement to a fine man and as a tribute to two special people—you and your brother—who led me back to God." He seemed to remember something. "And Cathy, you're not to help serve tonight. You are now my guest, not my employee!"

Cathy had never seen such a dinner. Winter roses graced the table that was laden with food fit for a king.

Mr. Evans had ordered enough of the fine food so that all the servants might have the same meal in their dining room. *Since he has returned to God's fold, his generosity knows no bounds,* Cathy thought.

With the table grace offered by Edward and with Davis beside her, Cathy picked up her spoon to stir her tea. She dropped it with a clatter and gave a startled cry. The color drained from her face.

"What is it, my precious?" urged Davis, immediately on his feet.

"The spoon!" she pointed.

"Is something on the spoon?" worried Mr. Evans.

"Yes!" Cathy said. "The E."

"That's for *Evans*, Cathy," the old gentleman explained.

"Wait!" she cried and ran from the room.

"Go with her, Davis," ordered Mr. Evans. "She is ill!"

Davis found her in her bedroom ripping away the lining of the coat. "Cathy! Cathy!" He shook his head. "Today has been too much for my sweetheart."

"No, Davis, look!" She held up the spoon she had fished from the black coat's lining, an identical match to the one she had dropped on the table. "This spoon belonged to my grandmother. It is from the *same set!*"

Taking Davis's hand, she led him back into the dining room. "Can you explain this mystery, Mr. Evans?" she asked, holding up her spoon that was tarnished with time. "My grandmother had this spoon in her possession when she died."

"Your . . . grandmother?" The old fellow looked as though he'd seen an apparition.

"Catherine Willis."

"Then she *was* my Catherine! Willis was her maiden

name. You mentioned her when you came, and I followed every lead but could find nothing. When Catherine left—when I sent her away—she took half the spoons from our wedding set. This is the first time I've used them. I thought she'd . . . she'd be honored." The old man tried to drink in the knowledge with small sips. "But . . . they told me that Catherine died in the epidemic. And you say she was your *grandmother?*"

"If I am figuring right," spoke up Davis, trying to help solve the tangle, "you must be Cathy and Edward's grandfather!"

"The quilt Bonny had—?"

"It was my grandmother's, too."

"Yes, I recognized it. Why, I slept under that very quilt back in '47! Did you ever notice, Cathy, that the blocks make a perfect little cross up in one corner?"

"I hadn't noticed," Cathy said.

"I just figured someone donated Catherine's quilt to the poorhouse."

"I took it there myself. Bonny and I shared it."

"Cathy! I almost forgot!" Edward reached into his pocket and pulled out the brooch. "Matilda's husband said to give this to you if ever I saw you again. Matilda didn't want it; she said it was dreadfully outdated."

"Matilda's husband?"

"She married her cousin, Keeper Bates. How he came to have this, I don't know."

Mr. Evans's eyes, filled with a soft light of some yesterday, had not strayed from the brooch. "Turn the emerald over," he said. "On the back you will find some very small initials. I had that brooch made for Catherine as a wedding gift."

"Yes, there it is: J.D.E."

"Jerry Donald Evans. She called me Don. But we . . . we had no children, Catherine and I. That is, none that I knew of."

"Catherine's daughter was born in 1848."

"Oh, have mercy on my soul! I turned out my wife when she was with child!"

"She named her daughter Lia. That was our ma."

"*Lia.*" He savored the name on the tip of his tongue. "Yes, Catherine once said that if we ever had a daughter, she would name her Lia. Lia Catherine it was, wasn't it? Oh, Catherine, you brought me a daughter and I didn't know it!" It was a bittersweet cry. "But I must see her!"

"Our mother isn't alive, nor our father," Edward said. "But Grandfather Evans, you have two happy grandchildren sitting here. And you're all the family we have!"

Don. Cathy tried to resurrect some memory of her own in connection with the name, something that seemed urgent. *The note!*

"Grandfather! I found a note in Grandmother's purse to you."

"To *me?*"

"It said, 'Don, I have forgiven you.'"

A translucent glow came to his face. "It is more than I deserve! Now my life is complete—and the end is better than the beginning. I can go in peace! Come, my children!" He put an arm around each of them then directed his remarks to an unseen beloved: "Bless you, Catherine! Neither you nor God left me comfortless. You painted your most beautiful picture, my dear, in these two children.

"Just give me time, darling, to set my affairs in order and

place all I have into the hands of our grandchildren, and I'll come to you, Catherine. I have a feeling that it won't be long until we see each other again. Then we'll have a whole eternity together to make up for lost time. . . ."

As Davis's eyes held Cathy's, Edward quoted: *It shall come to pass, that at evening time it shall be light.*

"Amen." Grandfather Evans bowed his head. "Amen."